D0362273

# Violet's Hidden Doubts

## BOOK ONE
of the
*A Life of Faith:
Violet Travilla*
Series

Based on the characters by
Martha Finley

**MCP**
**Mission City Press**

Franklin, Tennessee

Book One of the *A Life of Faith: Violet Travilla* Series

Violet's Hidden Doubts
Copyright © 2004, Mission City Press, Inc. All Rights Reserved.

Published by Mission City Press, Inc.

No part of this publication may be reproduced, stored in a retrieval system, or transmitted in any form or by any means — electronic, mechanical, photocopying, recording, or any other — without the prior written permission of the publisher.

This book is based on the *Elsie Dinsmore* series written by Martha Finley and first published in 1868 by Dodd, Mead & Company.

| | |
|---|---|
| Cover & Interior Design: | Richmond & Williams |
| Cover Photography: | Michelle Grisco Photography |
| Typesetting: | BookSetters |

Unless otherwise indicated, all Scripture references are from the Holy Bible, New International Version (NIV). Copyright © 1973, 1978, 1984 by International Bible Society. Used by permission of Zondervan Publishing House, Grand Rapids, MI. All rights reserved.

*Violet Travilla* and *A Life of Faith* are trademarks of Mission City Press, Inc.

For more information, write to Mission City Press at 202 Second Avenue South, Franklin, Tennessee 37064, or visit our Web Site at: **www.alifeoffaith.com.**

### For a FREE catalog call 1-800-840-2641.

Library of Congress Catalog Card Number: 2002103832
Finley, Martha
    Violet's Hidden Doubts
    Book One of the *A Life of Faith: Violet Travilla* Series
    Hardcover:     ISBN-10: 1-928749-17-8
                ISBN-13: 978-1-928749-17-2
    Softcover:     ISBN-10: 1-934306-01-0
                ISBN-13: 978-1-934306-01-7

Printed in the United States of America
6 7 8 9 10 11 — 10 09 08

# —FOREWORD—

*M*ore than a century-and-a-half ago, Miss Martha Finley (1828-1909)—a former schoolteacher who became a best-selling author of Bible-centered fiction for children and adults—penned a novel about the life of Elsie Dinsmore, a young girl growing up in the pre-Civil War South. Miss Finley intended to write just one book about her heroine. But the response to her first Elsie story, published in 1868, was so overwhelming that she eventually wrote twenty-eight more, plus a companion series about Elsie's cousin Millie Keith.

Although Miss Finley never had children of her own, she possessed a remarkable understanding of the hearts and minds of young people and their struggles to live their Christian faith in a world filled with challenges and temptations. During her life, Miss Finley's works provided inspiration, hope, and guidance to millions of readers throughout the United States and abroad. When her final Elsie novel was published in 1905, however, tastes in reading had changed, and her wonderful stories of faith and courage were almost lost to new generations. Then in the 1990s, Mission City Press undertook the adaptation of Miss Finley's stories for modern readers, launching *A Life of Faith* books with *Elsie's Endless Wait* in 1999. Since then, eight Elsie Dinsmore novels and eight Millie Keith books have been published by Mission City Press.

Now the tradition continues with the first of a new *A Life of Faith* series focused on Elsie's middle daughter, Violet Travilla. *Violet's Hidden Doubts* begins in 1877 and picks up the story of Elsie and her family several months

after the conclusion of *Elsie's Great Hope* (the eighth book in the *A Life of Faith: Elsie Dinsmore* series.) For readers who haven't yet met Violet Travilla and her family, the following background should be very helpful.

## ❧ VIOLET TRAVILLA: A NEW HEROINE ❧

Violet was born in London, England—the third child of Elsie Dinsmore Travilla and her husband Edward. Her arrival was especially joyful because the family was enduring, as were all their fellow Americans, the tragic consequences of the Civil War. Family members were fighting on both sides in the war, and letters from home brought heartache upon heartache to the family. From Shiloh to Gettysburg, beloved brothers, uncles, cousins, and friends were dying in battle. Vi's birth on a sunny June day in 1863 was like a pledge of renewal to the troubled family.

The Travillas were wealthy Southern plantation owners. They opposed slavery and supported the cause of a united nation, but they also loved the South. When the Civil War began, the Travillas and Vi's grandparents were visiting in England. Their first impulse was to return to their homeland, but their families in the United States urged them to stay in England until the War's end. So Vi, as she's called, was two years old before she first set foot on American soil.

After the War, the Travillas went home to Ion—Vi's father's plantation located near a Southern seaport city on the Atlantic coast. Violet's grandfather, Horace Dinsmore, Jr., and step-grandmother, Rose, live at The Oaks, a plantation close to Ion. Vi's great-grandfather, Horace Dinsmore, Sr., lives at nearby Roselands plantation with his widowed daughter Louise Conley and her children. The

# Foreword

Travillas have a large circle of family and friends in their rural community and are highly respected for their Christian faith, kindness, and the ethical treatment of their employees, many of whom are former slaves. Edward Travilla is a hero to many for his battle to rid the region of the racist Ku Klux Klan during the Reconstruction period (*Elsie's Tender Mercies*).

Vi has six sisters and brothers. Missy is the eldest—age 20 at the time this novel opens and recently engaged to marry. Vi's elder brother, Ed, is 18. Vi (age 14) is next, followed by twin brothers, Herbert and Harold, who are 11. The two youngest Travillas are Rosemary (7) and Danny (3 1/2). Another sister, Lily, died after a long illness, when Vi was 11 years old.

In 1869, when Vi was almost 6, the Travillas became the guardians of Elsie's cousins, Molly and Dick Percival. The young Percivals had experienced a number of personal tragedies, including a terrible accident that cost Molly the use of her legs. Molly has now become a successful writer of stories, and despite seven years' difference in their ages, Vi and Molly are very close friends.

As *Violet's Hidden Doubts* opens, life at Ion is very busy for the Travillas. Though they have many servants, the children are expected to help with chores; they make their beds, clean their bedrooms and their classroom, and assist their mother and their nursemaid, Aunt Chloe, with other household tasks. Missy, Ed, and Vi also care for their younger siblings when an extra hand is needed.

The children are schooled at home by their parents. Vi studies languages and literature, mathematics, history, and science. Like most girls of her time, she is also learning to sew and embroider. She and her sisters take lessons in

piano and in drawing and painting. Though not musically gifted like her mother, Vi is artistic and loves to sketch the beautiful scenery around her home. The Travilla children enjoy plenty of outdoor activities—riding horses, playing games, and exploring the countryside. Vi gets to travel more than most children of her time—trips to her mother's plantation in Louisiana, summer holidays at the seashore, and visits to New York and Philadelphia.

No matter where the Travillas are, Bible study and prayer are regular parts of their daily life. Vi's parents, both devout Christians, have raised their children to love the Lord and honor His commandments. God is a living presence in all their lives, and they rely on Him to guide them through each day.

As a little girl, Vi was a lively and sometimes unpredictable child. When she was a toddler, she had the habit of sleepwalking, but to everyone's relief, she grew out of it. She has always been an imaginative girl, curious to learn about the world and dedicated to her studies. She is very close to her father—in part because they share the same sense of humor and independent spirit—and it is he who helped her through her darkest time, when her sister Lily died. Vi is normally very forthright, but there are occasions when she tries to hide her emotions in order to protect others. Now a teenager, she is sometimes unsure of herself and uncertain about her future. Her faith in the love of her Heavenly Father is unshakable, but her belief in herself is not so secure and can cause her to feel... hidden doubts.

And now, Mission City Press takes pride in carrying on Martha Finley's legacy and welcoming readers to Violet Travilla's exciting life of faith.

# Travilla/Dinsmore Family Tree

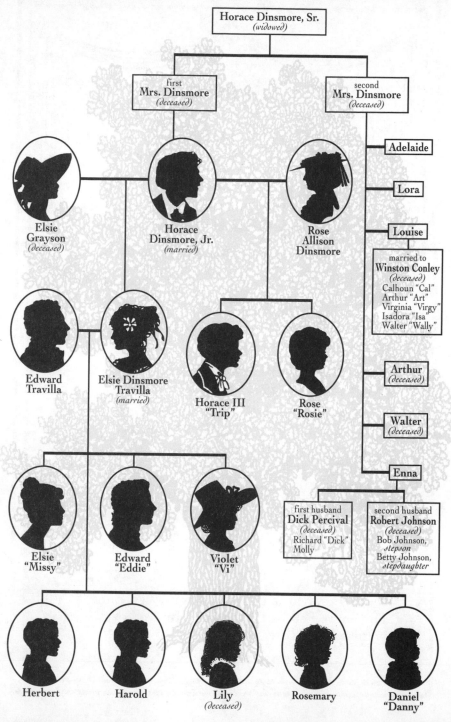

Horace Dinsmore, Sr.
*(widowed)*

first
**Mrs. Dinsmore**
*(deceased)*

second
**Mrs. Dinsmore**
*(deceased)*

Elsie
Grayson
*(deceased)*

Horace
Dinsmore, Jr.
*(married)*

Rose
Allison
Dinsmore

Adelaide

Lora

Louise

married to
**Winston Conley**
*(deceased)*
Calhoun "Cal"
Arthur "Art"
Virginia "Virgy"
Isadora "Isa"
Walter "Wally"

Edward
Travilla

Elsie Dinsmore
Travilla
*(married)*

Horace III
"Trip"

Rose
"Rosie"

Arthur
*(deceased)*

Walter
*(deceased)*

Enna

first husband
**Dick Percival**
*(deceased)*
Richard "Dick"
Molly

second husband
**Robert Johnson**
*(deceased)*
Bob Johnson,
*stepson*
Betty Johnson,
*stepdaughter*

Elsie
"Missy"

Edward
"Eddie"

Violet
"Vi"

Herbert

Harold

Lily
*(deceased)*

Rosemary

Daniel
"Danny"

## SETTING

$\mathcal{T}$he story begins in October of 1877 at a Southern plantation known as Ion, the home of Violet Travilla and her family.

## CHARACTERS

### ∞ ION PLANTATION ∞

**Elsie Dinsmore Travilla**, Violet Travilla's mother and the wealthy daughter of Horace Dinsmore, Jr.

**Edward Travilla**, Violet's father and owner of Ion plantation

Their children:

> **Elsie** ("Missy"), age 20; engaged to Lester Leland, an artist studying in Italy and the nephew of family friends
>
> **Edward** ("Ed"), age 18
>
> **Violet** ("Vi"), age 14
>
> **Herbert** and **Harold**, twins, age 11
>
> **Rosemary**, age 7
>
> **Daniel** ("Danny"), age 3 ½

**Molly Percival**, age 21, and her mother, **Enna Dinsmore Percival Johnson** (Horace, Jr.'s youngest half-sister)

**Aunt Chloe**—Elsie's faithful maid and companion, and **Joe**, her elderly husband

**Ben**—Edward's valet and lifelong friend, and his wife, **Crystal**, the head housekeeper at Ion

**Christine**—nursemaid to Rosemary and Danny

**Enoch**—a farm worker

## ∞ THE OAKS PLANTATION ∞

**Horace Dinsmore, Jr.**—Violet's grandfather, owner of The Oaks plantation

**Rose Allison Dinsmore**—second wife of Horace Dinsmore, Jr. and mother of Horace ("Trip") Dinsmore III and Rosie Dinsmore

## ∞ ROSELANDS PLANTATION ∞

**Horace Dinsmore, Sr.**—Violet's great-grandfather, a widower; owner of Roselands plantation

**Louise Dinsmore Conley**—widowed daughter of Horace Dinsmore, Sr., and mother of:

> **Cal**, age 29, manager of Roselands
>
> **Art**, age 25, a physician
>
> **Virginia**, age 23
>
> **Isa**, age 21
>
> **Walter**, age 20, a cadet at West Point

## ∽ Viamede Plantation ∽

(Elsie Travilla's plantation in Louisiana)

**Mr. and Mrs. Mason** — Viamede's chaplain and his wife

**Mr. Spriggs** — the plantation manager

**Aunt Mamie** — longtime housekeeper at Viamede

**Mrs. Maureen O'Flaherty** — a new employee

## ∽ Others ∽

**Dr. Barton** — retired family doctor and close friend of the Travillas and Dinsmores

**Dr. and Mrs. Silas Lansing** — an eminent surgeon and his wife

**Dinah Carpenter** — granddaughter of Chloe and Joe; now living in New Orleans with her husband and young children

**Mr. and Mrs. Mayhew** — a New Orleans lawyer and his wife

**Mrs. Duke** — a mission volunteer

**Richard** ("Dick") **Percival** — Molly's brother; a recent graduate of medical school in Philadelphia

**James Keith** — a young minister from the Midwest

**Louis Embury** — owner of Magnolia Hall, a plantation near Viamede; a widower with two daughters, Corinne and Maddie

**Dr. Bayliss** — a physician who serves the people of Viamede plantation

# CHAPTER

**1**

# Bruised Feelings

*Then Jesus said to her,
"Your sins are
forgiven."*

LUKE 7:48

$\mathcal{V}$iolet Travilla sat at her bedroom window, looking down onto the circular driveway and gazing at her Papa. Edward had just returned from his early morning ride and was drawing his horse to a halt near the entrance to Ion. As Vi watched, he dismounted and handed the reins to a stableman. Edward patted the young man on the back and said something that brought a broad smile to the stableman's face.

*Papa is so handsome,* Violet thought, *even at his age, and Eddie looks more like him every day. Oh, dear, I must stop thinking of my big brother as "Eddie." He gets so annoyed by that name now. He is* Ed *Travilla, and I must remember to call him what he wishes. It's a good thing that Missy doesn't ask me to forget her nickname, too, though my darling big sister will be changing her name soon enough. Mrs. Lester Leland—Elsie Eugenia Travilla Leland—that will be our dear sister's name when Lester returns from Italy and they are wed. So many changes in our lives.*

Vi sighed and rose languidly from her seat. *Too many changes*, she thought as she went to her dressing table and took up her brush to give her dark, shining hair one last smoothing. She caught her reflection in the mirror and stared at herself. This was not an act of conceit. Quite the opposite. Violet, at fourteen, considered herself the ugly duckling of her family. The face that looked back at her seemed to hold none of the beauty of her mother's and elder sister's. Even her little sister, Rosemary, though only seven, was clearly blessed with their mother's ringleted hair, delicate complexion, perfect features, and clear hazel eyes. Despite the passing years, her mother, Elsie Dinsmore

Travilla, was still regarded by all as a great beauty (although, as Vi well knew, her mother cared very little about such things).

Vi contemplated her hair. *It curled when I was little*, she thought, *and now it is as straight as an old stick. How did that happen? And how did I grow so tall? Oh, I'm not sure I want all these changes. Why can't I look like Mamma and my sisters? Why do I always have to be so different?*

In the mirror, her deep-brown eyes flashed back at her with self-reproach. "You have no reason to envy anyone," she told herself firmly. "Hasn't our Heavenly Father commanded us not to covet and warned us against the sin of envy?"

She turned away from her image and resolutely squared her slim shoulders. She strode to her desk and made a neat pile of the books and papers she would need for her studies. She was especially careful to include the neatly penned French lesson that she was to recite to her mother that day. Then she moved to her bed, took up the small Bible she had been studying earlier, marked her place with a ribbon, and gently set the book on her bedside table. Closing her eyes, she raised a brief but earnest prayer, asking the Lord to help her accept herself as she was and to resist all jealous thoughts. Refreshed by the understanding that He would give her strength, Vi hurried from her room.

Her family was already gathered at the table when she entered the dining room. Her father had just seated her mother and was now helping young Danny into the high chair that all the Travilla children had used when they were toddlers. Danny sat on one side of his mother and Rosemary at the other. Missy was seated at the center on the far side of the long table, with the twins, Harold and

Herbert, like bookends on either side of her. Vi's own place was on the near side of the table, between her brother Ed, who held her chair and complained in a joking tone that his eggs were growing cold, and Molly Percival, the dear cousin who had come to live with the Travillas nearly eight years earlier, after the accident that crippled her. (Molly's mother, Enna, now also resided at Ion with the Travillas, but she usually had breakfast in her room.)

Vi slipped into her seat quickly. Her father, having settled Danny in the high chair, took his own place at the end of the table opposite his wife. Immediately all heads were bowed and Edward said the blessing over the meal.

Breakfast began and everyone was soon eating and conversing about their plans for the day. As the hands on the mantel clock moved to the half hour, Ben — Edward Travilla's valet and trusted friend — entered the room. He carried a large stack of letters on a small tray. Ben said "Good morning" to the family and was warmly greeted in return, as Edward began to sort through the mail — a ritual followed every day for as long as anyone could remember.

There were a number of letters for Elsie and Edward. Two envelopes were passed to Ed — one an invitation and the other from a school friend. Molly was handed several envelopes — all, it appeared, from the publishers of her stories and translations. Rosemary, the twins, and even little Danny each got a note from their grandmother, Rose Dinsmore, who saw them almost daily but understood the joy that receiving letters brings to young children. At the bottom of the stack was a fat envelope addressed to Missy.

As he passed the letter to his eldest child, Edward said with a twinkle in his eye, "This seems to carry the scent of

salt air and sea water. Perhaps it has journeyed across an ocean to find you, Missy dear."

The young woman blushed prettily and smiled as she took the envelope. "I hope it had a pleasant voyage," she said, gazing at the bold handwriting of the address—the same artistic hand that had signed a large still-life painting which hung above the sideboard in the dining room.

"Since you seem to have eaten your fill," Edward said, "I think your mother will agree to excuse you now, Missy. You may wish to read Lester's letter in privacy."

Missy turned to her mother with a question in her expression, and Elsie nodded with a smile. Missy stood and hurried from the room with the light and lively steps of one who thrives on love.

Edward returned to the mail. After a minute more of shuffling through the letters, he looked at Violet. Those who did not know him might have thought his face was marked by grave disappointment as he said to his middle daughter, "It seems that you and I have been left out, Vi."

"But you have lots of letters, Papa," Vi protested.

"Ah, there you are mistaken, my pet. I have lots of bills to be paid and business queries to answer," he said, "but not a single line from friend or relative to gladden my heart."

"Nor do I, Papa," Vi snapped. "But I would rather you not announce it to everyone. They don't have to know that I've been left out," she added sharply.

Vi hung her head, but not before Edward saw tears glistening in her eyes. Surprised, he looked to his wife at the other end of the table. Elsie seemed as bewildered as he, but she did not comment. Preoccupied with their own letters, no one else noticed Vi's little outburst or the look of concern that passed between her parents.

Recovering himself quickly, Edward said in his light-hearted style, "I think we are all done now, so everyone may be excused. I have a little business to attend to, and I'm sure that the rest of you could use a few extra minutes to review your lessons before your classes with Mamma. We shall all return here at nine for morning devotion."

There was a general rustling of chairs as the Travilla children stood—remembering to thank their parents before scattering to their rooms. Ed, who at eighteen was as tall and nearly as strong as his father, lifted Molly from her seat and carried her easily to her wheeled chair; he pushed the chair, accompanying his cousin out to the veranda for a breath of the clean autumn air. At the sound of feet exiting the dining room, Danny's nursemaid, Christine, entered to take her young charge away to have his hands and face thoroughly washed.

Alone, Edward and Elsie expressed their mutual astonishment at Vi's behavior.

"Her remark to you was rude, as was her tone," said Elsie, "but I do not believe she intended any disrespect."

"Nor do I," Edward agreed. "In fact, the disrespect was mine. I teased her in front of her brothers and sisters, and I should have known better. Vi's resilience and genial humor have always hidden a deep well of sensitive feelings. I must admit that I cannot get used to the fact that she is growing up and that I must be more thoughtful."

Elsie said, "I, too, have difficulty realizing that our Vi is becoming a young lady."

"No longer our little fairy," Edward replied with a gentle smile. "But I must make amends to her and cultivate the habit of biting my tongue when I am tempted to tease."

Then an idea struck him. "Would you allow her to miss school this morning?" he asked.

"At your request, I would," his wife said, putting her hand lovingly upon his arm. "But what do you have in mind?"

"I was thinking that she might enjoy a father-and-daughter day. I have to go to the west field where the men are clearing that old oak grove. It's a good ride there and back, and the day is clear and warm. Vi might enjoy an outing and a picnic."

"And some concerted attention from her adored papa," Elsie smiled.

"I hope she will like that, too," Edward said. "I shall enjoy some time alone with her even more."

Elsie squeezed his arm and looked into his handsome face. "You are so much alike, you and Vi," she said. "I realized many years ago that should there ever be conflict between the two of you, it would come from likeness rather than differences. And like you, Vi cannot stay angry for very long. By all means, ask her to join you today. An outing will be good for you both."

Vi had gone straight to her room after breakfast. She sat on her bed and dabbed at her eyes with her handkerchief.

"What a silly goose you are, Violet Travilla," she said sternly to herself. "Papa meant no hurt to you. He was only teasing, and you were dreadfully rude."

Just the thought of her father brought a fresh rush of tears, and her face burned with shame. She wiped at the tears, struggling to banish them.

"You must apologize," she said with determination. "That's all there is to it. You must not let Papa leave the house until you have said that you are sorry and asked for his forgiveness."

She went to her mirror, as she had done earlier that morning, but this time she saw only her red-rimmed eyes and flushed cheeks. She found a fresh handkerchief and was wiping away the last traces of tears when she heard a soft knock at her door.

She hesitated for a moment, hating to see anyone until all signs of her distress had been erased, but then she said, "Come in."

She was still looking into the mirror when she saw the door open behind her and her father reflected in the silvery glass. Instantly, she turned around and ran into his open arms.

"I'm so sorry, Papa," she sobbed, "for what I said and how rude I was. I don't know why I acted that way. I never meant to hurt your feelings."

Edward hugged her close and began softly, "I accept your apology, pet, and I hope you will accept mine. I was wrong to tease you, and especially wrong to tease in front of others. I had no right to embarrass you. The truth, dearest, is that I spoke before I thought."

He pulled a handkerchief from his pocket, and raising Vi's face, he patted the soft cloth against her cheeks.

Vi looked into his eyes and saw that they were full of love. She struggled to control her crying, taking in several large gulps of air to steady her voice and calm the trembling sensation in her stomach.

"But, Papa," she said at last, "I like your teasing, for you are never cruel or thoughtless. I don't know why I got upset this morning. I had no reason to feel embarrassed or to talk back the way I did."

Edward slipped one arm around her shoulder and guided her to the narrow bench that stood in front of her window. Together, they sat down, and he kept his arm about her.

# Violet's Hidden Doubts

"You're becoming a young lady," he said. "You will be fifteen on your next birthday. At your age, we all have new feelings, and our emotions sometimes rule our heads. It's a natural part of growing up. Perhaps you might have phrased your complaint more politely, but I should have realized that my casually spoken words could cause you pain. I am not so old yet that I should forget how I felt at your age."

Vi looked sideways up at her father, and a little smile tugged at the corners of her mouth. Her rich brown eyes, now dry of tears, sparkled. "You're not old, Papa," she said. "At least, not *so* very old."

Edward sat back, as if in surprise. "Why, Vi," he exclaimed, "I am but a spring chicken! A mere pup! Whatever do you mean—not so very old?"

"Well, not as old as Grandpapa, though he is your best friend," she replied with mock seriousness, "but older than Mamma, and much, *much* older than I."

He laughed, and at the sound of it, Vi felt a weight of guilt lift from her heart. Edward's laughter was to her among the sweetest, most reassuring sounds in life.

"I don't think that I want to grow up, Papa," she said. "Everything seems so complicated now, and I worry about things that never bothered me before—silly things like not getting a letter this morning. The older I become, the more mistakes I seem to make, like being rude to you because I didn't get a letter."

"Again, dearest, that's natural. The secret is to see each mistake we make as an opportunity to grow in wisdom and to learn from all that we experience. Things do get more complicated as we grow older, but when we are wise, we can recognize our errors and ask for the forgiveness of our

10

Heavenly Father and of those we may offend. And with wisdom, we can forgive others as our Lord forgives us."

"Then you really forgive me, Papa?" she asked.

"Of course, I do," he answered. "And will you forgive me?"

"I do," she said, adding, "though my impertinence was the worse fault."

"Then all is settled between us, and we will both ask our Father for His forgiveness. Now we must make amends. I shall try to be more thoughtful and understanding if you try to be less quick to take offense," he said, squeezing her shoulder as she nodded her head in agreement.

"So let us speak no more of it," he went on. "I have what I hope will be a happy suggestion. I must go out to the west field, and as it is such a beautiful fall day, I thought you might accompany me. If you change to your riding habit now, we can leave right after devotion and prayers. Your mother has agreed that you may have a holiday from your studies, if you like."

"Oh, dear," Vi said in confusion.

"If you have a more important engagement…"

"Oh, no, Papa. Not an engagement. It's just that I have a French lesson with Mamma today, and I have worked very hard on my pronunciation. I'm not sure if…"

"Don't worry yourself, pet," Edward said cheerfully, though in truth he felt a twinge of disappointment. "We can go tomorrow. The clearing of that field has been slow and will continue for several days more. Today, I'll work with the men, but tomorrow I promise to be your attentive escort. If we ask her politely, I'm sure that Crystal will prepare a delicious meal for us, and we can enjoy a ride and a picnic. What do you say?"

"That would be perfect, Papa," she agreed with enthusiasm.

"Then tomorrow it will be—unless you receive a better offer," he said.

"You're teasing me again, Papa," Vi giggled. "What better offer could there be?"

Edward hugged her to his side. "You must allow me a little teasing, dear girl, for it is a habit of mine that I cannot break easily. We shall keep it just between us."

Vi reached up and grasped the strong hand on her shoulder. "Please, Papa, don't ever change. Promise me that you won't," she said in a near-whisper. Edward, who was closely attuned to the natures of each of his children, caught the genuine seriousness that now infused her tone.

"I shan't, pet," he said. "I will always love you from the fullness of my heart and be here for you until the end of my days."

They sat for a minute more in silence—father and daughter bathed in the golden light of the autumn morning—and Vi drew confidence, as she had since she was an infant, from the strength of her Papa's love. Then Edward took his watch from his pocket, and he saw that the time was but a few minutes before nine.

"May I escort my lovely daughter to the dining room for our devotion?" he asked with exaggerated formality.

"You may, kind sir," Vi replied in the same manner. They rose, and Edward took her hand and put it upon his arm. As if she were the most regal princess of Europe, he led his daughter from the room.

# CHAPTER

# Lessons in Love

*The entire law is summed up
in a single command: "Love
your neighbor as
yourself."*

GALATIANS 5:14

*A*s soon as the morning's devotion—which included all the members of the household staff—was concluded, each person went to his or her daily duties. Edward, with Ben at his side, rode out to the fields, while Elsie and the younger children gathered in the schoolroom. Molly went to her room where she would spend the morning at her writing. Young Danny was having a romp in the garden, under Christine's watchful eye.

From the youngest to the eldest, each person in the large, well-run household felt the comfort of the familiar—knowing that work was being done, chores were attended to, and life was proceeding according to their expectations.

Ed, who was entering one of the great Eastern universities in just a few months, was taking advanced studies with a tutor in the city. He left the house shortly after his father and would not return until the afternoon. Missy usually assisted her mother in the schoolroom, but the receipt of her fiancé's letter excused her on this day.

In the kitchen, Crystal and her helpers were busy preparing the midday meal. Aunt Chloe, still spry in her seventies, was making her morning visit to the servants' quarters, checking on the health and well-being of every employee and putting together a mental list of their needs. Old Joe—far less mobile than his wife but no less sharp in mind—directed the housemaids about their work. Beds were made, dishes washed, laundry gathered, furniture dusted and polished, ashes raked, and logs laid in all the fireplaces. The jobs that kept the house and plantation humming and productive were being tended to as usual on this altogether ordinary Tuesday morning. Not in their wildest imaginings could anyone have guessed what the rest of the day would bring.

In the schoolroom, Vi was focused entirely on her French recitation. She had, as she told her father, been working very hard on her pronunciation. As she waited her turn for Elsie's attention, she silently mouthed each word in the lengthy recitation, forming her lips and tongue to shape the foreign sounds with precision. Nothing that was happening around her penetrated her concentration. Vi herself often marveled at this ability to concentrate so intensely on her studies, when her thoughts seemed so confused at other times.

Finally Elsie called Vi forward, and the girl declaimed the entire passage — selected from the work of a French philosopher — to near perfection. Elsie was more than pleased. She offered several suggestions to enhance Vi's pronunciation, but on the whole could do little more than offer praise. Elsie's pride increased as they discussed the contents of the difficult passage. Vi had not only learned the words correctly but had also delved into their meaning, and her comments were remarkably astute for one of her age. Vi glowed with satisfaction at her mother's praise.

Brought into the schoolroom by Christine, Danny crawled happily onto Elsie's lap and asked for the story of Goldilocks and "the twee bears." All the children, including Vi, gathered round to listen.

"So what do you think of Goldilocks, Danny?" Elsie asked when she finished the story.

"She's a wude girl," Danny said with great conviction. "She ate the bears' bweakfast and slept in their beds and didn't even ask!"

"Maybe she doesn't have a mamma and papa as good as ours," Rosemary said, "to teach her the right way to treat others."

"Not that we're so perfect," Vi responded, thinking of her own rudeness that morning and again feeling regret.

"Vi is right. None of us is perfect," Elsie said, "and that's why we are so grateful that the one who is perfect, our Lord Jesus, taught us the ways to show love and respect for our fellow men. Would you like to hear a story that Jesus told us about love for others?"

"Yes, please," Danny replied, snuggling against his mother.

"It's from the tenth chapter of Luke," Elsie began. "One day, a man asked Jesus about the command to love our neighbors as we love ourselves. The man wanted to know who his neighbor was. So Jesus told him about another man who was traveling from Jerusalem to Jericho when he was attacked by thieves. The thieves took away everything he had, beat him, and left him lying half-dead beside the road. Soon a priest came down the road, but seeing the beaten man, the priest crossed to the other side and walked on. Then another man, a Levite, happened down the same road. And he saw the beaten man, but he also crossed to the other side and walked past."

Two red circles had appeared on Danny's chubby cheeks. He said forcefully, "That's so bad!"

Elsie said, "The man must have looked terrible—like a beggar or even a thief. Would anyone have the love to help him?"

"I don't know," Danny said in a small whisper.

"Well, a man from Samaria came by. We don't know his business there, but Jesus tells us that the Samaritan had a donkey and money. Surely he had no need to stop, but the Samaritan took pity. He cleaned the man's wounds and took him to an inn. The Samaritan stayed with the man until the next day. When he left, he gave money to the innkeeper so that the man would be cared for until the Samaritan returned. Now who is the real neighbor?"

"The man with the donkey!" Daniel exclaimed.

They laughed, and Elsie patted her little boy's head. "That's right, Danny. The Good Samaritan didn't think of himself. He showed mercy to someone in need, and Jesus tells us, 'go, and do likewise.'"

Vi said nothing, but she closed her eyes and tried to imagine what she would have done. *Would I have been afraid and run away? Would I have thought only of myself?* She pictured the Samaritan hurrying to the wounded man. *The Samaritan did not think about himself. Oh, dear Lord, help me to be like the Samaritan! Help me to put the needs of others before my own selfish wishes. Help me to be a loving and merciful person.*

When Vi opened her eyes, the other children were discussing the parable. Rosemary commented thoughtfully, "If Goldilocks was a Good Samaritan, she wouldn't go into the bears' house and sleep in their beds and eat their food."

Elsie smiled as she listened to the children's spirited conversation, and Vi understood why. Elsie and Edward had taught their children to see the Lord's teachings as the great blueprint for their earthly lives.

*In joy and in sorrow,* Vi thought, *as Mamma says, the answers to life's questions are all in God's Holy Word.*

As the morning came to an end, the young Travillas began to tidy their desks. They were almost done when Missy entered. She went to her mother and said, "Molly and her mamma have already eaten, for Aunt Enna seemed quite hungry after her walk. But Papa hasn't returned yet, and Crystal asks if you wish to delay lunch until he arrives."

Elsie considered for a moment, then replied, "No, I think we will begin at the usual time. Your father said that he might eat with the men." She looked at the little watch pinned to her blouse. "Please tell Crystal that we'll be down in fifteen minutes, Missy dear. And take Rosemary to wash her hands."

Missy got her little sister; Herbert and Harold, too, went to prepare themselves. Danny was playing with a slate and some chalk, and Elsie was putting the lesson books back on the shelf when Vi came to her side.

"Mamma, I want to apologize for my behavior at breakfast," Vi said softly. "I was rude to Papa and no less so to you, for my remark showed disrespect."

"Did you apologize to your father?" Elsie asked.

"Yes, ma'am, and we talked before he left. He was so understanding," Vi said.

Elsie smiled. "Yes, he is. He has an uncanny ability to put himself in the shoes of another and understand not just the behavior but its causes as well. You and your brothers and sisters are most fortunate to have a father like Edward. And I also accept your apology, dearest."

Vi put her arm around her mother's waist and hugged her. "Thank you, Mamma. I try so hard to keep my feelings

to myself, but it is as though they escape me no matter what I do."

"But, Vi, we do not expect you to hide your feelings," Elsie said. "Papa and I are here to listen to you and help you in every way we can. And no matter what you feel, you can always take it to your Heavenly Father."

"I know that, Mamma, but my feelings seem so small and petty sometimes. It seems wrong to take them to God when others have so many terrible problems."

Elsie stepped back and put her hands on her daughter's shoulders, which were level with her own now. She looked straight into Vi's beautiful, troubled eyes and said, "God bears all our burdens and relieves our suffering. Nothing is too small for Him, and you should never hesitate to speak to Him. Do you remember these verses from Matthew 10? 'Are not two sparrows sold for a penny? Yet not one of them will fall to the ground apart from the will of your Father. And even the very hairs of your head are all numbered.' Vi, not even the hairs on your head are too small for the Lord's attention. He wants to hear all your thoughts and troubles and to help you at all times."

Vi dropped her gaze. "I often think my worries are too unimportant for Him."

"Well, child, I can tell you that you are incorrect. Nothing is too trivial for Him. Take all your worries and concerns to God, and He will give you His love and strength and guidance. He may not help or answer you in the way you hope or expect, for His wisdom is beyond our comprehension, but He will always do what's best for you. Trust Him always."

Vi raised her eyes again and replied, "Love and trust are inseparable, aren't they, Mamma? I know that I love God

and He loves me, so I must trust in His love no matter what—even when it is difficult."

Elsie smiled warmly. "Knowing that is a sign of great wisdom, Vi. Keep the promise of Psalm 32 with you, that the Lord's unfailing love surrounds those who trust in Him. Keep faith with Him, my dearest girl, for He always keeps faith with you."

"Thank you, Mamma," Vi said simply, though many thoughts suddenly filled her mind. A new understanding of the meaning of trust seemed to have burst upon her, and she realized that she had much to talk over with her Heavenly Father and Friend.

At that moment, however, small hands tugged at both Elsie's and Vi's skirts, and mother and daughter looked down into a bright, chalk-covered face.

"I'm hung-wee," Danny said.

"Of course you are, my darling," Elsie laughed, sweeping him up in her arms. "But first we must find a damp cloth and wipe the chalk from your nose and cheeks. Vi, you go ahead, and my dusty boy and I will join you in a few minutes. We can talk more this evening if you like."

"I would like that very much, Mamma," Vi replied.

---

Luncheon was served though Edward had not arrived. As they ate, the children talked about their activities for the afternoon. Herbert and Harold were to have a riding lesson. Missy requested permission to take the buggy and go into the city to do a few errands (chief among them, though she didn't say so, to mail her return letter to Lester), and she asked if Rosemary and Vi might accompany her. Rosemary's

face lit up at the idea of an excursion, but Vi declined, saying that she wanted to do some pencil sketching outdoors. Elsie herself announced that she would be going to The Oaks and that Danny would go with her—Molly and Aunt Enna, too, if they wished.

Vi did want to sketch that afternoon. She loved the colors of early autumn and was planning to do a series of watercolor paintings of locations about the plantation—works that she hoped would be good enough to present to her parents for Christmas—and her sketches would be her starting point. But she also had a lot of thinking to do. Her earlier conversation with her mother had stirred new ideas about the nature of trust, and she wanted to talk with both her parents. She hoped that she might be able to have some time with her father when he returned.

In fact, she expected him to come into the dining room at any minute, for she had not heard Elsie say that he might stay in the field all day. The meal went on, and when he had not appeared as dessert was being served, Vi began to feel a little anxious. *Perhaps he will work till day's end*, she thought. *He sometimes does. Then he'll be tired, and I may not be able to talk to him until tomorrow.* If there was a hint of selfishness in her concern, it was not intentional. Vi was sensitive to her father's well-being. She had teased him that morning about his age; in truth, however, she'd become increasingly aware of how much Edward worked, and she sometimes worried that he pushed himself far too much. He was always so willing to take on tasks that might easily be assigned to others.

Despite his youthful looks, Edward was in his late fifties, and to Vi, this was an age when her father should begin to rest from hard labor. But Edward often said that to be able to work was one of God's gifts, and he reveled in days like

this, when he shared the physical labor of farming with his employees. But Vi, always the most sensitive of the Travilla children, never failed to notice when her father seemed fatigued or his endless supply of good humor was a trifle low. As the others ate their desserts and chatted on about their activities, she raised a quick, silent prayer — *Thank You, Lord, for my Papa, and please watch over him and help him in all his hard work* — before turning her attention back to the apple custard that had been placed before her without her even noticing.

Everyone had just been excused and Vi was about to leave the dining room when her mother called her back.

"You seemed unusually quiet during lunch," Elsie said. "I hope you're not still worried about the matter of this morning."

"I was just thinking of different things. I've been hoping that Papa would be back this afternoon."

"Ah, I see," Elsie smiled. "There are times when a girl just needs to talk to her father. When I was your age, my own Papa was the world to me. Even now, there are times when I simply need to talk things over with him. That's one of the reasons I'm going to The Oaks this afternoon. Are you sure you won't join us for the ride?"

"No, ma'am, unless you desire me to," Vi said. "I really want to sketch today. The light is so clear, and I want to work on some drawings of the boathouse and landing at the lake."

"The day is most definitely a brilliant one for those with an artist's eye," Elsie agreed. "I will give your grandparents your

love. But don't stay out too late. The weather turns chilly rather early now, and I don't want you to catch a cold."

Elsie kissed Vi and went to the rear of the house to invite Molly and Enna on the ride to The Oaks. Everyone else had scattered, so Vi left to get her drawing supplies from her room. The prospect of an afternoon of drawing cheered her. *The sun will chase away my dark thoughts*, she told herself as she climbed the stairs in the main hall—taking them two at a time as she used to when she was a little girl.

No one was near the front door when a horse and rider charged up the driveway at full gallop. The rider pulled the horse to a rearing halt and, dropping the reins to the ground, dismounted even before the horse had stopped.

Breathing rapidly, Ben dashed inside and looked about. Seeing no one, he ran down the entrance hall and into the dining room. Crystal, his wife, was there, checking that the table was clear of all the dinner things. She looked up at her husband and instantly recognized the import of his dreadful expression.

"What's happened?" she asked.

"Got to find Miss Elsie," he gasped. "Mr. Edward's been hurt, and they're bringing him back now, in the big cart. Got to find her."

Crystal grabbed his shoulders. His face was covered with dust but she saw two tracks—the mark of tears—that ran from his eyes across his checks. She put her hand gently to his face.

"I'll get Miss Elsie," she said. "She was planning a ride to The Oaks this afternoon, but I don't think she's left yet.

You stay here and catch your breath. Whatever the news, you got to have your wits about you when you tell her."

"Then go quickly," he said, waving her hand away. "Just don't let the children hear you."

"How bad is it?" Crystal asked even as she crossed to the door.

"Don't know exactly," he answered in a breaking voice. "I sent one of the boys to fetch Dr. Arthur at Roselands. But I could see it was bad. Real bad."

Crystal was gone before the last words left his mouth.

# CHAPTER 3

# Trouble in the Field

*In this world you will have*
*trouble. But take heart!*
*I have overcome*
*the world.*

JOHN 16:33

# Trouble in the Field

*A*t about the time Violet and her siblings were sitting down to their meal, the men in the west field of Ion were just returning to their work. They had stopped for food — cold, roasted meat and corn cakes brought from the quarters that morning, hot coffee brewed over a campfire in the field, and water from barrels hauled to the site in a large farm cart, which had also carried the saws, axes, and other tools required for the work of clearing.

Edward ate with his men, and they talked about the work underway; then Edward asked each man about his family, especially the children. Edward Travilla was their employer, but to many of the men he was also a friend. Some, like Ben, had known Edward all their lives; most of the workers, however, had come to the plantation after the Civil War and emancipation. Among the former slaves of the region, it had become known that the owner of Ion was a just and fair man who paid good wages and wasn't afraid to get his own hands dirty when there was hard work to be done. Edward's reputation had gained as well from what was still called the "Battle of Ion"—the brief but tumultuous conflict that had rid the area of the Ku Klux Klan a decade earlier. In the years since, Ion had attracted a highly capable and loyal workforce, and Edward always repaid the loyalty of his employees in kind.

Their task that afternoon was felling an enormous oak tree that would have to be cut into parts before it could be hauled away. The tree was old and large, and the undergrowth was dense with bushes and thick vines. There was always the danger of accidents, but the men were both cautious and

29

experienced. Edward joined his men as they assembled at the oak tree. The line of its eventual fall had been calculated, and the tree was rigged with a network of ropes that would be used to pull it down into a clear space.

His shirt sleeves rolled up tight around his strong, tanned upper arms and his face streaked with dirt and sweat, Edward grabbed one side of the saw. A man named Enoch, a match to Edward in size and strength, grasped the opposite handle in his large, gloved hands. Back and forth they drew the saw, ripping into the wood until the blade neared the midway point. Another pair of men stood by, but Edward and Enoch carried on, the rhythm of their movements in perfect unity. It appeared they might attempt to finish the job.

Suddenly, there was a low sound almost like a moan that seemed to come from the earth itself. The moaning quickly rose to a high-pitched scream. Edward and Enoch appeared not to hear, but the other men recognized the noise. The weakened old tree was splitting at some point inside. As the tree's groaning and shrieking increased, the shouts of human voices joined the chorus, and several men rushed forward to pull Edward and Enoch away from the saw. They all had to run, for there was now no way to know how the great tree would fall.

Edward, backing away from the tree, shouted an order to the workers manning the guide ropes. He hoped they might be able to pull the tree to the right position. He looked around to locate the other men, seeing that all were headed for safe areas.

Watching from some distance, Ben yelled frantically, "Get outta there, Mr. Edward! She's coming down!" The huge oak was beginning to sway and buckle under its own weight, and Ben could see that it would crash not in the direction the men expected, but in the area where Edward now stood.

Hearing Ben's voice, Edward at last turned. Behind him, he heard a roaring crack like a cannon blast, and he knew that he must run for his life. He did run, praying as he did that all the men were clear. But then he encountered a stretch of rough undergrowth, thick with snake-like vines that grabbed at his feet and threatened to drag him down. The cracking and splintering noises were now like a barrage of gunfire, and as he forced his way forward, Edward felt, rather than heard, the shifting of earth as if the ground itself were heaving under his feet. Then the air was sucked from his lungs. With a horrible *whoosh*, the tree toppled.

Ben saw it happen. Edward running; the tree falling as if in pursuit of him; then Edward vanishing in a cloud of green and gold and brown as the tree hit the ground with a terrible, awesome thud. The ground shuddered with the blow. Then, except for the gentle quivering of the tree's dry leaves, there was silence.

In seconds, Ben, followed by other workers, reached the place where he had last seen Edward—though Ben always said later that time seemed to stand still in those moments. But the tree's mighty limbs and the dust raised by its fall obscured their vision. The men began searching, and some-one called for handsaws to cut away the larger branches. Someone else yelled for quiet so they might listen for a voice, but no call for help was heard.

"Where are you, Mr. Edward?" Ben cried out in desperation as he tore at the branches and leaves. Seconds later a deep voice called, "Here! He's here!"

Ben raised his gaze and saw the powerful figure of Enoch standing not many feet away. Enoch was waving an

axe above his head as if it were a flag, and the searching men scrambled toward him.

Edward lay still, his face to the ground. He was trapped at the fork in a large branch, and its two thick fingers pinned down his legs and torso. Ben moved swiftly but with great gentleness to lift Edward's head and clear his mouth of dirt. Putting his own face close to his fallen friend's, Ben felt a soft, unsteady flow of air. Edward was breathing but unconscious.

Instantly, saws and axes were put to work to remove the huge limb. When it was severed from the tree, Enoch and several others bent to lift it. With strength that seemed beyond human capabilities, Enoch held the limb above the ground, enabling the others to free Edward's limp form. With great care, the men moved Edward away from the spot, and only when Enoch saw that all were beyond danger did he release the limb. It fell with a crash that eerily echoed the thundering collapse of the giant oak.

Two of the men had removed one side from the farm cart and brought it to where Edward now lay. A rough blanket was spread atop the long, flat, wood rectangle, and steady arms lifted his body again, placing him on the makeshift stretcher. Ben could see that Edward's leg was broken, and he called for someone to bring straight branches for a splint. Another man tore his own shirt off and ripped it into strips to bind the splint. They worked hurriedly. No one said anything, but all the men shared an understanding that Edward's injuries were likely to be much graver than a broken leg.

The splint completed, the men lifted the stretcher and bore it back to the cart. The mules had been hitched, and the driver was in his seat, ready to depart at Ben's signal.

Ben climbed into the cart and knelt beside his friend just as Edward opened his dazed eyes. Ben offered words of comfort as Edward slowly came to awareness.

"You'll be all right, Mr. Edward," Ben said. "We're takin' you up to the house, and I already sent young Gus to Roselands for Dr. Conley. You'll be fine, I just know it."

Edward's mouth moved as he attempted to speak, and Ben tried to quiet him.

"Don't say nothing, sir. Save your strength now."

But in a harsh whisper, Edward forced the words out— "Tell...Elsie. Go...tell...Elsie."

Ben understood immediately. "I will," he said. "I'll go straight to the house."

Ben looked up and motioned to someone standing nearby. Enoch climbed into the cart and came to Ben's side.

"Now, Enoch's going to sit with you while I ride on up to the house," Ben said to Edward. "Enoch's going to make sure you have an easy journey back home. Don't you worry, Mr. Edward."

Edward looked into his old friend's eyes and tried to smile. But even that small effort contorted his ashen face with pain, and his eyes fell shut once more.

Enoch took Ben's place beside the stretcher, and Ben quickly got down from the cart. He went to the front and consulted with the driver, warning the man to proceed slowly lest the bumping of the vehicle cause further injury to its passenger. Tears began to stream from Ben's eyes as he hurried to mount Solomon—Edward's horse—and spur the animal to a gallop.

# Violet's Hidden Doubts

By a stroke of good fortune, both Dr. Arthur Conley and his brother Cal were at Roselands when Gus rode up. Without dismounting, the young Ion worker called out to see them, and so apparent was the urgency of his demand that an old servant standing on the portico steps rushed inside without asking a question.

Arthur and Cal appeared just moments later, and Gus told them what had occurred. Cal asked for more details of the accident while Arthur ran back into the house to get his medical bag. He summoned one of the housemaids and dispatched her to the stable. Within five minutes, Arthur's and Cal's saddled horses were being led to the house.

Arthur then instructed the stableman who had brought the horses to take the fastest steed available, ride for Dr. Barton, and escort the old physician to Ion. The little housemaid had joined the anxious group, and Cal told her to take Gus inside and inform old Mr. Dinsmore of the accident. To Gus, Cal said, "Try not to alarm our grandfather too much. He has not been well, so there is no need to speculate about Edward's injuries." Cal then instructed Gus to ride to The Oaks to inform Horace, Jr. of the events.

The maid spoke up: "I'll take care of your grandpa, Mr. Cal. I'll see that he isn't too much disturbed."

"Thank you," Cal said. "You will have to speak to my mother as well. Tell her that she is to stay here with Grandpa until we have more news."

"You can trust me, sir," the young woman said. "I'll handle Miss Louise. We'll all be praying for Mr. Edward as hard as we can."

Gus arrived at The Oaks about a half hour later, and much the same events were repeated. As soon as Horace Dinsmore heard the report, he ordered that his horse be

brought, then hurried to tell his wife of the accident. They decided that Rose should follow him to Ion as quickly as possible, bringing what they would need for an extended stay.

"God willing, Edward's injuries are not serious, and we shall not be required there for long," Horace said. He clasped Rose's hands to his chest and closed his eyes. "Let us pray, love. Whatever has happened, Dear Lord, give us the strength to support Edward and our daughter and grandchildren through this time of trial."

"And the wisdom to accept Your will, Dear Father, whatever it may be," Rose added in a voice that trembled poignantly.

---

When Horace, with Gus at his side, galloped up the drive to Ion, they were greeted by the incongruous sight of the large, weathered farm cart standing before the gracious entrance to the plantation house. Coming closer, they saw many men, including Ben and Cal Conley, gathered near the cart. Horace's daughter was in the wagon, bent low over her husband as Arthur Conley ministered to the inert figure lying on a panel of rough boards.

*Is he dead?* Horace thought desperately as he left his horse and pushed through the men to a place beside Cal near the rear of the cart.

As if in answer to his question, he heard Arthur saying, "We're going to take you inside now, Edward. We will try to cause you as little pain as possible."

"All is ready for you, my dearest," Elsie crooned to her husband. "You will soon be off this hard board and in bed."

# Violet's Hidden Doubts

Then she stood, and her cousin Cal reached out, put his hands around her waist, and lifted her from the wagon to the ground. Seeing her father there, Elsie swayed slightly, and he took her in his arms. Horace could feel her shaking, as she had when she was a child and afraid, but her spine was straight and she showed no sign of fainting. Instead, she grasped his hand and held it tightly as she watched her husband being moved.

The men, Enoch in the lead, took over—sliding Edward's pallet from the cart and hoisting it down in one swift, sure movement. Five of them, two on each side and one at the foot of the wooden stretcher, bore it up the front steps and into the house.

# CHAPTER 4

# Whose Fault?

*My heart is in anguish within
me; the terrors of death
assail me.*

PSALM 55:4

# Whose Fault?

*V*i had watched everything from her bedroom window. The mules, held tightly in check by one of the field workers, pulling the farm cart ever so slowly toward the house. The farm hands walking in silence behind the cart. Her mother and Ben running to meet the cart and then walking alongside it until it came to a stop at the entrance to the house. A powerful man in the cart lifting her mother up, and then her mother down on both knees, bending over the still figure that lay there. Arthur and Cal Conley riding at full gallop up the drive.

With a rising sense of dread, Vi watched and listened to the voices below her. Cousin Arthur's voice, her mother's — snatches of their low talk: "unconscious…" "clean break…" "don't want to move him yet…" "my darling…" Vi could see her father's body and Arthur's hands touching it. She could see her mother's back and, when Elsie turned her head, the drawn look of her face in profile, but not her father's face.

Vi leaned as far out of the window as she could. But still her father's face eluded her. *Oh, to see his face for a second! To see his face and to know that he is alive. If I could just be sure he was alive, I could move from this spot and do as I was told. It's like a nightmare! Maybe that's all it is,* Vi thought frantically, *just a horrible nightmare that I will wake from at any moment.*

When Ben had broken the news to Elsie, she'd immediately asked Crystal to find Vi, Missy, and the other children right away and send them to the nursery. Catching Vi as she was about to leave the house, Crystal had said only, "Your Papa's been hurt, and your Mamma wants you to keep the little ones in the nursery. Now don't you worry. It'll be all

right. Just go on up and wait till your Mamma can get to you. It'll be just fine." And Vi had dutifully gone back upstairs, but not to the nursery.

Despite Crystal's assurance, Vi knew instinctively that something was terribly wrong. So she ran to her room, drawn back to the same window from which she had watched her father ride up the driveway that very morning, laughing and sharing a joke with the stableman. Edward's expression from that morning floated before her eyes — his face so alive with the simple pleasure of his ride. She could see again the motion of his hand as he patted the stableman's shoulder in comradeship.

*Oh, God, at least let me see him move!* her mind cried out. *Let me see some sign that he is alive!*

Directly below her window, Old Joe had come out on the veranda, and one of the workers had joined him. Vi could not see the men but she could hear them clearly.

Joe asked what happened, and the other man replied, "That big, old oak fell while Mr. Edward was cutting it. Came down like thunder and caught him before he could get clear. Broke his leg, I know, but…"

"But what?"

"But it's worse than that, Joe. I've seen men hurt before, and this is bad."

"We don't know that," Joe said forcefully. "We can't know nothing like that till Dr. Conley tells us. You and the men — don't you be spreading any stories before we get the truth from Dr. Conley."

"We ain't, Joe," the other man protested. "But you oughta know that it could be bad."

"I'll believe it when I hear it from the doctor or Miss Elsie — and not before."

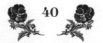

Then they stopped talking. But the words tore at Vi's mind and heart—*could be bad.*

She wanted to scream at the invisible men below her: *How bad? Please just tell me how bad!*

With her eyes glued to the wagon, she struggled to hear more. All the while, the most dreadful thoughts hammered at her. *If he dies…my fault…if I'd only gone…if only…it's my fault. God, save him! It's all my fault!*

Then she saw her father's hand move. Or did it? Yes, her father's hand had moved, and her mother had taken it in her own.

A voice spoke behind her, and Vi jumped at the sound.

"You come away from that window, Violet," Aunt Chloe was saying. "I need you in the nursery now, like your mamma said."

Grabbing the old nursemaid tightly, Vi exclaimed, "Papa's alive! I saw his hand move!"

"Sure he's alive," Chloe replied, keeping her own fear out of her voice. "And if you wanna help him, you come along with me and stay with your brothers and sisters and just wait for your mamma."

Taking the girl's trembling hand, Chloe led her across the room. Vi didn't resist. In truth, she had little sense of what she was doing. Her body seemed to move without her being conscious of it. All she could think of were the words she had uttered—*Papa's alive!*

---

Under Arthur's supervision, the men had taken Edward inside and gently moved him onto the bed in one of the back

rooms. Arthur slipped a pillow under Edward's head, and Crystal drew the covers up.

The men watched for a few moments, and then, without a word, they stood back as Elsie entered, followed by her father. Still in silence, the workers raised the empty stretcher and departed.

Elsie took her husband's hand but sought Arthur's eyes. Reading her unspoken question, Arthur said, "He has lost consciousness again, but his breathing is more regular. From my examination and what Ben tells me of the accident, I'm sure Edward has not suffered any head or spinal injury. His leg is broken, but it is a clean break and I've set it. I also believe several ribs are broken, yet his lungs sound clear, so I will bind his chest. But..." He hesitated.

"But there may be injuries you cannot see," Elsie said, completing his thought in a voice so firm and strong that it surprised everyone in the room.

"Yes," Arthur said simply. "I sent for Dr. Barton, and he should be here soon to consult."

"Is there anything we should be doing?" Elsie asked.

"I must bind his ribs, and I can use Crystal's assistance. Then we must keep him still. The risk is that any movement may cause a damaged rib to puncture a lung."

Elsie turned to Horace, "You will stay here, won't you, Papa? I must go to the children, but I will not be long. Then we will keep watch together."

"Of course," Horace replied. "And yes, you must hurry to the children. They are surely terrified for their father and only you can give them the comfort they need. But Rose will arrive shortly, to care for them. She and I will stay as long as you and Edward and the children need us."

He went to her and placed his arm around her shoulder. Elsie stood very still, holding her husband's hand, and she was calmed by her father's embrace. A part of her longed to break down and let her tears flow and wash the overwhelming fear from her body. Yet the stronger part of her knew that now was not the time for weeping. As Edward had always been her rock in times of trial, so she must be doubly strong for him and their children. Until Edward was restored to them all, she must be both mother and father.

Rose Dinsmore's carriage had pulled up to the portico not long after Edward was taken inside. When she entered the house, Rose found Old Joe sitting in a chair in the hallway. The old servant struggled to rise, but Rose bade him to remain seated.

"Stay where you are, Joe," she said kindly. "Where is Mr. Edward now?"

"They took him into the back bedroom, the one next to Miss Molly's room," Joe replied. "Miss Elsie is with him, and Mr. Horace and Dr. Arthur."

"And the children?"

"They was all about to go off when Ben brought the news, so they know what's happening—that their papa's been hurt. Miss Elsie told everybody to go up to the nursery and wait for her. Chloe's there, too. But Mr. Ed, he's not home from the city. I expect him right soon, and I thought maybe I best stay here in case he needs me."

"Yes, do wait for him, Joe. And when you see my husband, please tell him that I have arrived and gone to the children."

"I'll surely do as you ask, Miss Rose," Joe said. "I'll keep a lookout, and while I'm sittin', I'll pray with all my heart

for Mr. Edward to get well. I can't think what we'd do with-out him, Miss Rose. I just can't bear to think of it."

Rose tried to reply, but the words caught in her throat. So she lay her hand on the old man's arm in a reassuring gesture that she hoped might comfort them both.

If Rose had expected tears when she entered the nursery, she was surprised. The young Travillas were quiet and solemn but dry-eyed. Herbert and Harold sat at the play table, for which they were both too large now, with Rosemary between them. The three were working a picture puzzle—the boys encouraging their little sister to find the pieces and guid-ing her progress. Near the fireplace at the end of the room, Missy sat in a high-backed armchair with Danny on her lap. In soft tones, Missy was reading her baby brother a story, and Danny curled against her and sucked his thumb. Nearby, Chloe was in a rocking chair. Her two hands clasped an old black Bible to her breast, and she seemed to be drawing strength from the mere touch of the book. The last to catch Rose's attention was Vi, who sat in the window seat, her feet drawn up and her arms clasped around her knees. Her face was pale and expressionless as she stared out the window.

At Rose's entrance, the children looked to her for news of their father, and Rose felt a hot wave of helplessness pass over her. She could not give them the answers they longed to hear.

An uneasy moment went by before Harold spoke, "Is Papa all right?"

"Can we see him?" Herbert added.

Moving to the little table, Rose said, "Your Cousin Arthur is with him now, and Dr. Barton is on the way. I

wish I had more news, but I haven't seen your Papa. Yet I know that Arthur and your mamma and grandpapa are taking very good care of him."

Rosemary suddenly jumped up from her seat, her chair tumbling over behind her.

"Is he dead?" she screamed, running to Rose and burying her face in her grandmother's skirt. "Is my Papa dead?" she sobbed.

Rose bent to cradle the child. "Oh, no, Rosemary darling. Your papa is not dead. Believe me." She lifted the girl up in her arms. Stroking Rosemary's curls, she gently began to sway as if she were soothing an infant. "Your Papa is alive, and your Mamma is taking good care of him, just as she cares for you when you are sick. God is watching over your papa. God loves your papa, and He will do what is best for him. God loves you, Rosemary, and all of us."

Rosemary's sobbing seemed to subside a bit, and in a small, choked voice, she said against her grandmother's shoulder, "I want my Mamma. I want Mamma."

Still rocking the child in her arms, Rose said to them all, "Your mamma will be here soon. And we must be very strong for her. Your papa and mamma need your strength and your courage, children. Can you be very brave and wait until she is able to come here to us?"

"Yes, Grandmamma," Herbert and Harold replied.

"I'll be brave, too," Rosemary said in a whisper, though she clung to her grandmother more tightly than before.

Chloe had risen from her chair, and she motioned for Rose to take her place. Gratefully, Rose settled herself and Rosemary in the sturdy old rocker. Herbert and Harold followed and sat on the floor beside Missy's chair, huddling

close to her as if to protect themselves against cold winter winds.

Only Vi remained apart from the group. From the window seat, she gazed upon her loved ones, but she felt incapable of moving. Her legs seemed to be made of lead, her arms and shoulders of solid stone. Inside this body of metal and stone, her heart raced. She wanted to cry — to sob as Rosemary had done — but her eyes were dry, so dry they burned. She knew that Papa was alive, but what did that mean? Over and over, she heard the words of the farm worker: *Could be bad. Could be bad.*

Vi listened as Missy began to pray aloud, followed by Rose and the twins and even Rosemary, and Vi wanted desperately to add her own words. She wanted to join her family in their expressions of hope, to share their fears and be warmed by their embraces. But this body of stone and lead would not allow her to move. She was like a prisoner held back by impenetrable walls and bars. *How can I take comfort from my family when I am the reason for their sorrow? How can I ever tell them that what happened was my fault — that I could have prevented it?* Each guilty thought hammered at her brain, and her head throbbed. But far worse was the pain that gripped her heart with its icy fingers.

Vi's head dropped forward until her forehead touched her knees, and she began her own soundless, solitary prayer: *Lord, please, please,* she begged. *Please make Papa well and strong again. Please don't let him die like this. Have mercy on my family and do not take him away from us. Oh, please, Heavenly Father, save our Papa!*

CHAPTER

5

# The Vigil Begins

*Even though I walk through
the valley of the shadow of
death, I will fear no evil,
for you are with me.*

PSALM 23:4

# The Vigil Begins

*N*ot long after Rose's arrival, Elsie made her way to the nursery, and even Vi roused herself to find shelter at her mother's side. Elsie gathered her children close and explained what had happened. She told them what Ben had said, that their father had refused to run until he saw that all the other men were safe. She explained his broken leg and ribs. She did not, however, speculate about other injuries, for there was no need to raise fears without reason.

Missy asked about Dr. Barton, and Elsie said that the doctor had reached the house just as she was coming upstairs.

"But why does Papa need two doctors?" Vi asked, for this news fueled her growing fear that her father's condition was worse than anyone dared say.

"Well, Dr. Barton is one of our oldest and dearest friends, and he was our family doctor for many, many years before he retired. He would want to be called," Elsie replied. "Dr. Barton has a great deal of experience, and we all value his knowledge and his judgment."

"Can Papa talk to us?" Herbert inquired.

"He's sleeping now, and sleep is good for him," Elsie said. "But I did speak to him when he was first brought to the house, and he wanted me to tell all of you how much he loves you. He is counting on you to be very strong."

"I want to see my Papa," Rosemary said softly. "Can I, Mamma?"

Elsie touched her daughter's soft, warm cheek and smiled: "Not right now. We do not want to wake him, no matter how much we wish to hear his voice. I cannot tell you exactly

when you may see him, for we must do as Cousin Arthur and Dr. Barton think best. But you can help Papa if you will."

"How, Mamma?" Harold asked.

"Well, I want you and Herbert to help Grandmother Rose and Aunt Chloe and take charge of the nursery," Elsie said.

"Of course, Mamma," Harold agreed.

"But is there nothing else for us to do?" Herbert asked in a plaintive tone.

"For the time being, that is what I need of you boys," Elsie said. "Missy, I'd like you to come downstairs and keep watch for Ed."

"Yes, ma'am," Missy said, glad of this task. She had been worrying about her brother, and she wanted to be with him when he received the news of their father's accident.

Looking to her middle daughter, Elsie said, "Will you come too, Vi? I'd like you to sit with Cousin Molly and Aunt Enna. They know what has occurred, but I am afraid Enna may become upset. Enna always enjoys your company, and you may be able to assist Molly as well."

Vi nodded her agreement. She felt better, somehow, because her mother expected her to help someone else. Her own emotions were in such a frightening tangle. If she was with Molly and Aunt Enna and if together, they all prayed very, very hard for her Papa—then maybe her secret feelings of guilt and shame would fade away.

"And me, Mamma?" Rosemary was asking.

Rose spoke up, "I'm counting on you to watch over Danny, dearest."

And so the young Travillas were given their assignments—in part because Elsie knew how much they wanted to help and that it was important for them to feel

that they were doing something for their father. She also genuinely needed their assistance, especially that of the older children.

"The most important thing we can do," Elsie said, "is to pray for Papa. When we are together and when you are alone, lift your prayers to our Heavenly Father. Speak from your hearts, my children, and He will hear you and give you comfort. Shall we all pray now?"

"You say the words, please, Mamma," Rosemary begged.

Elsie led them in a prayer of hope. Edward was the focus of her tender words, but she asked God's guidance as well for Arthur and Dr. Barton. She offered thanks for Ben and Enoch and the rest of the men who had rescued Edward. She prayed for God's mercy: "We are afraid, Heavenly Father," she said, "and we seek Your grace and strength to help us and our beloved father and husband and friend through this crisis. You, Lord, are our song and our salvation, an ever-present help in times of trouble. We cry out to You to hold us all in Your strong arms as we pass through this dark valley. Please, blessed God, fortify our faith. Comfort us so that we may comfort one another. Restore Edward to health and to our loving arms."

Then she recited the familiar words of Psalm 23, and everyone joined in. Elsie's eyes were closed, but she felt the warmth of her children, her stepmother, and her devoted Chloe surrounding her as if a great blanket of love enfolded them all. She heard the quality of their love and faith in their voices. So revived was she by the prayer and the closeness of her family, Elsie did not notice the absence of one voice—nor did she recognize the strange quality of pain and fear in Vi's dark eyes.

# Violet's Hidden Doubts

Ed arrived at Ion, and Missy informed him of their father's accident. Together, they went to the nursery to comfort their siblings. Meanwhile, Vi was sitting beside Enna on a comfortable settee in Molly's room. Vi's head rested on Enna's shoulder, and the woman gently patted the girl's dark, silken hair.

Vi, of course, knew only a little of her great-aunt's past. Enna had been severely injured—and her mind impaired—in an accident when Vi was young, so to Vi, her Aunt Enna had always been Molly's strange, childlike mother. Then, less than a year ago, Enna had almost drowned in Ion's small lake, and she had lain in a coma for more than a week. When she at last "came back," as Molly always said, Enna was changed. While still childishly simple in many ways, she was almost always rational now and kind and thoughtful to everyone. What's more, Enna had become a Christian, opening her heart in love and gratitude to the One who had restored her to life and to her family.

Vi dearly loved her great-aunt and her Cousin Molly, and she often sought out their companionship. Her affection for Molly was owed in part to respect for the fact that Molly, despite her physical handicap, had thrown off self-pity and was determinedly making a life for herself and her mother. Molly was a published writer of growing repute. She loved all the Travillas but had a special affinity for Vi. She admired the girl's spirit and intelligence, and she understood Vi's frustrations as well.

"Mamma wanted me to comfort you," Vi was saying. "But it is you who give me comfort."

"That's what family is for," Molly said.

Tears began to trickle from Vi's eyes. "I don't know what we'll do if... Papa..."

"I think it is never wise to anticipate outcomes over which we have no control," Molly said thoughtfully. "You know that Cousin Arthur is doing his best for Edward right this minute."

"And Dr. Barton," Vi said.

"Dr. Barton is a fine man," Enna remarked in a dreamy kind of tone. "He helped to save my life, you know. Saved me twice."

Enna continued to hold Vi close and caress her hair, but Molly could see that her mother had drifted back to another time and place—a time when Enna had been the patient and her life hung in the balance.

Molly rolled her wheeled chair forward, took Vi's hand, and spoke softly: "I know that you're afraid, but you must not let yourself be overwhelmed by your fears. Neither you nor I nor anyone can know what will come to pass, for only God can see the future."

In halting phrases, Vi tried to say what her heart longed to reveal. "But I should have...if I'd...but I didn't..."

"What did you fail to do, dear girl?" Molly asked. "You didn't prevent your father's accident? But you had no way to do so. Even had you been there on the spot, you could not have changed what occurred. You musn't blame yourself, Vi. No one understands better than I the harm that guilty feelings can do."

Vi looked up suddenly, and her eyes were full of questions. *Does she know? Does Molly know what I did?*

Molly continued gently, "For a very long time after the accident that took away the use of my legs, I lived in a land of resentment and fed myself on thoughts of 'might have'

and 'should have.' I blamed myself, and I blamed Mamma. I spent so much time blaming that there was nothing left over for healing. I was so full of fear and anger and guilt that I made everyone miserable, most of all myself."

Vi had not heard this before, and she couldn't imagine her cousin ever being the bitter person Molly was describing. As she listened to Molly, Vi forgot her own secret sorrow. She asked what had changed Molly's heart.

"After Mamma's first accident, your father and mother brought me into this house to live. They loved me and let me have my grief. But most important, they introduced me to Jesus. With His love and your parents' help, I began to see that I could not reclaim the past. I will never forget one remarkable night—I was reading the Bible with your mother, and we came to a passage in the Book of Isaiah. The words almost leapt from the page at me: 'Forget the former things; do not dwell on the past. See, I am doing a new thing! Now it springs up; do you not perceive it?'"

Molly paused, and then continued tenderly, "At that moment, I understood somewhere deep inside myself that God wanted me to stop thinking about what might have been and let Him do something new. I had no notion of what it was, but I knew that I could do nothing if I kept myself chained to blame and regret."

Molly squeezed Vi's hand lovingly and then shifted her position so that her back rested more comfortably against her chair. "My situation was not the same as yours, Vi, but I do know that we cannot move forward if we are endlessly looking back. We may lament the past, but we cannot undo what has been done, for that is not in our power."

"I know," whispered Vi. "I must think only of Papa now. But...but I'm so afraid. I want him to be well again, but what can I do?"

Enna had been listening to their conversation more closely than either Molly or Vi suspected. "Hope and pray," she said suddenly. "We must pray together."

"Yes, Mamma, we must," Molly said. Leaning forward again, she reached toward Vi with one hand and her mother with the other, and they were linked in a small circle. Molly began to speak, and as the sweet words of hope flowed from her, Vi opened her heart to the source of all consolation. For those minutes, the dark shadow was lifted. But it did not disappear — not yet.

As afternoon wore into evening and evening into night, a strange quiet settled upon all of Ion. If anyone had wandered into the star-sprinkled darkness, going from the plantation house to the workers' quarters and on to the tenant houses that lay scattered far and wide, he would have heard few of the sounds of normal life. Dogs barked, horses neighed and stamped in their stalls, and cattle lowed in the pastures. But the usual sounds of human activity — the laughter and quarreling of children, the chatter of adults as they completed the tasks of the day, the whistling of night visitors returning to their homes — were absent. Sharp ears, however, might have picked up a low hum of prayers coming from house after house. Sharp eyes would have seen that the lights burned late into the night in the church in the quarters. Here and there, voices were joined in soft and solemn hymns.

# Violet's Hidden Doubts

The stillness that affected all the residents of Ion was repeated at Roselands, The Oaks, and beyond. News of Edward Travilla's grave injuries had spread rapidly throughout the countryside, and there was no gaiety among his friends and neighbors that night. A man who had earned the respect of all and the friendship of many was in danger of being taken away from this close community, and few could bring themselves to contemplate such a loss. But where there is life, it is said, there is hope. Prayers of hope for Edward Travilla were raised by rich and poor alike, and even some who had lost the habit of praying found themselves in conversation with the Lord, asking for His mercy on the good man of Ion and all who loved him.

# CHAPTER

6

# Fears and Prayers

*Out of the depths I cry to you,
O LORD; O LORD, hear
my voice.*

PSALM 130:1-2

r. Barton's consultation with Arthur was lengthy and troubling. They thoroughly examined Edward, concluding that their friend and patient had suffered severe injuries to several vital organs. Dr. Barton recommended that they get a specialist's opinion, and Arthur readily agreed. So just before ten o'clock, Dr. Barton took his leave, but instead of heading for the comfort of his home, the elderly physician turned his buggy toward the city. There he would seek out Dr. Silas Lansing, an eminent surgeon of his acquaintance. He was determined to bring Dr. Lansing back to Ion with all speed.

It was left to Arthur to explain to Elsie and Horace. This he did with honesty and compassion. He also told them that Dr. Barton had gone to find Dr. Silas Lansing and would return as quickly as possible. Until Dr. Lansing could examine Edward, Arthur did not want to offer any prognosis.

"I am a country doctor," the young man said modestly, "and I'm aware of my limitations. As you may know, Dr. Lansing distinguished himself as a battlefield surgeon in the Civil War, and he is widely respected for his innovative surgical techniques. We are fortunate that he lives so close to us."

As she listened, Elsie's face grew pale, but she remained clear-eyed and attentive to her cousin's every word. Horace began pacing the floor, trying to absorb the implications of Arthur's words.

"I know that Lansing is a good man, and his professional reputation is excellent," he said when Arthur finished, "but are there others we should call upon? I think I ought to send one of the men to the rail station with a telegraph message for Dick Percival."

"What can Dick do, Papa?" Elsie asked.

"I do not intend for him to come here, dearest," Horace replied, "but his former teachers in Philadelphia are among the best doctors and surgeons in all the country. They might suggest others who specialize in such injuries."

"That's a good idea, Uncle Horace," Arthur agreed. "I doubt we can find better than Dr. Lansing, but every avenue should be explored."

Arthur turned back to Elsie and said, "I wish that I could give you more definite news, but you must not lose hope. Edward is strong in both body and spirit. I know of no man with a more intense love of life, and his dedication to you and his children is powerful. Even in my short career, I have seen how the will to live can work wonders."

"Thank you, Arthur," Elsie responded with a tiny smile. "Be assured that I have not given up hope. But may I return to Edward now?"

"Of course," Arthur said.

When she had gone, Horace had another question for Arthur. "Is there anything more I should hear?" he asked.

"No, sir," Arthur said. "I have told you and Cousin Elsie all that I know. I will keep nothing secret from either of you, or from Edward when he asks."

"As he surely will when he is awake," Horace said with a sad shake of his head. "Edward is my oldest and closest friend, and I cannot begin to adjust my mind to the possibility of losing him. But if that is God's will, we must accept it, and Edward will want the truth. I am absolutely confident that you will know what to say."

Arthur was gratified by his uncle's words, for he was all too conscious of his own lack of experience. "Thank you, sir," he said. "Now, shall we write your telegram to Dick?"

Dr. Barton had found Dr. Lansing at home and retired for the night. Dr. Barton made clear to the sleepy-eyed butler who answered the door that the situation was of great urgency. With a little prodding, the butler went to summon his employer.

After speaking briefly with Dr. Barton, Dr. Lansing hastened back to his bedroom to dress and gather his medical equipment. He also called upon his wife to locate a nurse whose skills the doctor valued highly and send a carriage to transport this nurse to the patient's plantation.

It was after midnight when Dr. Lansing and Dr. Barton arrived at Ion, only to learn that Edward's condition was worsening. He had been slipping in and out of consciousness, and his fever was rising, indicating infection. After Dr. Lansing had examined the patient, it became impossible to escape the conclusion that Edward's chances of survival were slim. His internal injuries were extensive, and the best the medical men could do was to keep him as free of pain as possible. It would soon be necessary, they agreed, to inform the family of the gravity of the situation.

Seeing the pain in Arthur's face, Dr. Lansing said, "I feel sure Edward will come through this night, so we need not speak to Mrs. Travilla yet. Let us tend to our duties and see how Edward progresses. We will know better in the morning. I do not believe in giving false hope, but neither do I wish to draw too hasty a conclusion."

Dr. Barton put a firm hand on Arthur's shoulder. "We will tell Elsie all that we know, for she deserves our honesty. But as Silas says, we cannot predict the outcome of Edward's illness. God alone possesses that knowledge."

It was nearing dawn when Edward awoke. Elsie saw his eyelids flutter open and leaned over to kiss his damp brow. His fever, which had risen during the night, seemed to have reached a plateau.

Dr. Lansing took Edward's wrist. The doctor counted the beats and after a few moments, he said to Elsie, "His pulse is steadier now. Let me lift his head, so you can give him water."

Elsie took a glass and gently held it to her husband's lips. With great effort, Edward managed one sip, then another. As the cool liquid entered his parched mouth, he tried to smile, but his eyes closed and he seemed to drift away again.

The doctor lowered his patient back onto the pillow, thinking the injured man had lost consciousness. But Edward's eyes opened once more, wide this time, and sought Elsie's face. She could see the fever that seemed to burn like a fire in his eyes, but Elsie realized that he was focusing on her.

"Oh, my darling!" she exclaimed in a voice breaking with emotion.

"I'm here," he answered in a slow, rasping tone that signaled the great effort each word required.

"Don't speak, my love," Elsie implored. "Save every ounce of your strength."

"I must," he said, his voice no stronger than a whisper. "I'll be going home soon. I'm ready, Elsie. Ready to meet" — he stopped and struggled to draw in breath — "my Savior."

She bent closer so that her cheek touched his. "If that is His will," she said softly, "but I pray it is not. I need you so much, my darling, my dearest love. Let me give you my strength so we can fight this infection together."

Faintly and with great effort, he said, "I want to live but I'm ready to die. Know that I love you and always will. Tell the children that I love them. Tell them to be happy because I will be happy. We will all be together again."

His eyes fell shut, and he seemed to sink deeper into the pillow.

Elsie instantly raised her panicked gaze to Dr. Lansing.

"He's only sleeping," the doctor assured her.

Elsie looked into her husband's beloved face — the face whose every line she knew as well as her own. She wanted to take him in her arms and enfold him in her own strength. *Oh, Dear Father in Heaven*, she prayed desperately to herself, *do not take him from us now. Help my beloved Edward fight for his life. Show me how to fight with him and for him — for without him, I do not know how to go on. Show me the way, Lord. Show me the way.*

Edward continued to sleep for several hours, and his sleep was almost peaceful compared to the restless, fevered unconsciousness of the night. As dawn broke and light began to seep into the room, his fever seemed to abate a bit under the constant, cooling ministrations of Elsie and the physicians.

# Violet's Hidden Doubts

Despite the urgings of the others that she rest, Elsie refused to leave Edward's side. And she was not the only one who kept a waking vigil. Rose and Chloe had gotten the younger children to bed and soothed them to sleep, but Missy, Ed, and Vi had refused all coaxing. They had gathered in Missy's little sitting room and talked and prayed throughout the night. With her sister and brother, Vi realized, she was better able to battle against the fear that threatened her.

Since her prayers with Molly and Enna, Vi had put aside the agonizing guilt that seized her when she first saw her father lying in the wagon beneath her window. As she prayed with Missy and Ed, Vi thought only of her Papa, and she began to believe that their hope was not in vain and that he would be restored to them. He would live through the night, she decided, and the new day would renew his strength. *Maybe it's not so bad as everyone says.* In her mind, she could see her Papa sitting up in bed, weak but getting better. She would be there with him, reading to him from one of their favorite books and helping her mother nurse him back to health. *If only I can pray hard enough…*

It was almost seven in the morning when Arthur came to Missy's room. He told his cousins that Edward's fever had leveled off and he was sleeping more easily. Getting through the night, Arthur said, was a good sign. But he wanted them to understand that their father was by no means out of danger and that it was impossible to say what would happen in the next hours.

"How is Mamma?" Vi asked.

"She won't leave your father," Arthur said, "but she's resting at the moment. Dr. Lansing's nurse arrived from the city and is tending Edward now."

Ed wanted to know when they could see their father.

"Perhaps when he wakes again," Arthur replied. "I know that your mother will want you there. But we're giving Edward potent medicine to help him sleep, for it is in sleep that the body can best heal itself."

He went on to explain Edward's internal injuries and Dr. Lansing's diagnosis. It was the most difficult discussion Arthur had ever had, but he knew that his cousins needed the truth. When he had finished, Vi asked the question that he so dreaded.

"Will Papa live?" she said softly, and the hope in her dark eyes nearly broke the young doctor's heart.

"I do not know," Arthur replied at last. "I respect you too much to give you false expectations. Your father's injuries are severe, and no surgeon alive has the skill to repair them. The infection is the worst danger. Edward is very strong, and his love for all of you is a powerful incentive to live. Dr. Lansing is probably the best physician in the country for this kind of situation. But truly, it is all in God's hands now. You must hold on to your faith, just as your father does."

As he spoke, the brother and sisters drew closer to one another. Missy's tears flowed freely, and Ed wrapped her in his arms as their father would have done. But Vi did not cry. Her face wore a blank look, but the light of hope in her eyes, which had shined so brightly just moments before, flickered out, and Arthur thought he had never seen such depths of pain before.

# Violet's Hidden Doubts

He took her hand. It was cold as ice. Arthur reached for a woolen shawl that lay on the couch and draped it around her. He knew Vi was in shock; all these dear young people were. He stood to leave, saying that he would have hot tea and toast brought up to them. A little sternly, he instructed them to eat and drink what he prescribed, for they must stay strong in body. Missy and Ed nodded in promise, but Vi didn't move. She was like stone, and Arthur resolved to return within the hour to check on her. With one last look at Vi's devastated face, he departed.

How many prayers were said that day is not possible to calculate. What had to be done on the plantation was done, but most of the work that normally occupied the people of Ion was suspended, and the church in the quarters became a gathering place for the workers and their families. The main house itself was eerily quiet as the servants went about their tasks. The children kept to their rooms and the nursery, as their mother requested—the younger ones huddling close to their grandmother and Aunt Chloe, while Missy, Ed, and Vi sheltered together and waited for more news of their father. Food was brought, and at Arthur's insistence, even Vi ate a little. The suggestion that they try to sleep was politely received and then ignored.

Just after midday, a rider arrived with a telegram from Dick Percival. Dick had sought advice from the best of his medical professors in Philadelphia, and they had all agreed that the most prominent physician available was Dr. Silas Lansing. Dick also stated that he himself was preparing to leave for Ion on the first train he could get.

Horace was truly grateful for Dick's efforts, though he had already settled his mind as to Dr. Lansing's skill. Horace conveyed the message of Dick's impending arrival to Molly and Enna, and he could not help smiling at the happiness in Enna's eyes when she heard that her son would soon be at her side.

Horace found himself almost envying Enna's gentle simplicity. He wished that he could know the peace of accepting whatever might come without question. But the thought of losing his dearest friend and of Elsie's and his grandchildren's grief and sorrow tore at his heart. *Strengthen me, Heavenly Father, for what lies ahead*, he prayed as he walked slowly back to the room where Edward lay. *Lift this frustration from me and let me feel the contentment that comes from accepting Your will. If You must take my friend now, help me to feel joy for him and for Your saving grace that will someday reunite us all in Heaven.*

# CHAPTER 7

# The Journey Home

*For to me, to live is Christ
and to die is gain.*

PHILIPPIANS 1:21

It had passed noon when Missy, Ed, and Vi heard steps in the hallway.

"It's Grandpapa," Ed said, recognizing Horace's familiar tread. He jumped from his chair and rushed to open the door.

Horace's face showed the strain of worry and lack of sleep, but his words were a balm to the young Travillas. "Your father is awake, and he wants to see you," he announced.

"Oh, is he well now, Grandpapa?" Vi cried out.

Horace hesitated a second before saying, "No, he is still very ill. But he is conscious, and he has asked for all of you. Go down now, while I get Rose and the little ones. Your mamma is waiting for you."

He started to leave but turned back. His expression was softened with emotion. "You must be strong, children. Your papa's fever has risen again, but he wants to see you before he takes more medication. Do not be dismayed by his weak appearance. Just remember that he is fighting very hard to recover. Be strong for him now as he has always been for you."

Horace's voice broke as he concluded, "Go to your papa, my dears, and…"

But he could not finish. He held his arms open wide, and his three grandchildren fell into his embrace.

There were a number of people in the bedroom when the young Travillas entered, but they saw no one except their

father and mother. The room was dim, for the curtains had been drawn and light came only from the oil lamps. But the windows must have been opened, for the room was cool and the air was fresh.

Edward lay absolutely still upon his bed, his arms extended above the light cover and his head raised slightly on a pillow. His face was pale and drawn, yet also spotted with the flush of fever. Elsie was gently pressing a cool cloth to his brow and temples and whispering to him.

When she sensed her children's presence, she looked up at them with a gentle smile that bid them to come forward. What fear they might have felt melted away in love and compassion.

"Missy and Ed and Vi are here, dearest," Elsie said to Edward. Then she rose so that her children might take her place beside the bed.

At the sight of them, Edward's face seemed to lighten. "My precious gifts," he said hoarsely. "My greatest blessings."

Vi longed to put her arms around him and cling to him as she had always done in times of trial. Instead, she laid her hand softly upon his, feeling his fever under her fingers. In the cool of the room, the heat of his skin shocked her, like touching a burning coal. But she didn't draw back. She would have braved a roaring fire just to feel his gentle touch once more.

"We're here for you, Papa," Ed said.

"We love you so much, Papa," Missy added.

"Pray for me?" Edward asked.

"Oh, yes, Papa, every minute since you were hurt," Missy replied.

With enormous effort, Edward focused his eyes on Ed. His mouth moved but he seemed unable to speak. The

nurse, who stood at the opposite side of the bed, put a damp cloth to his dry lips, and after a few moments, he was able to form the words.

"Ion will need you," Edward said to his son, "but not yet. Go on to school, Eddie. Learn and be wise for your brothers and sisters. You will be as father to them and right arm for your mother."

His speech faltered, and the nurse put the soothing dampness to his mouth again.

The full import of his father's words struck Ed with a sudden force that seemed to draw the breath from his chest. *He is saying good-bye*, the young man thought, and he wanted to shout in protest. Instead, he said, "I love you, Papa. I will do as you say."

"I love you, Eddie. I trust your good heart to do what is right always."

Edward's gaze shifted to his eldest daughter. "My first-born. So like your mother in beauty of spirit. Begin your life with Lester in joy and happiness, dearest Missy. I want you to be happy as Mamma and I have been. Walk always with our Lord. I love you, my daughter, and always will."

"And I will always love you, Papa," Missy said through her tears. "Always, always, you will be the finest part of me."

Edward's eyes closed. Vi, who stood nearest to him, her hand still covering his, did not dare breathe as she looked on her father. A single, frantic thought battered at her brain—*Don't go, Papa! Don't go!*

Edward lay motionless for several minutes. The nurse applied the damp cloth to his face and neck, and Dr. Lansing came forward to check his pulse. Otherwise, no one moved.

Then Edward's eyelids opened. He looked straight at Vi.

"Child of her father," he said. "We are alike, you know. You must follow your dreams, my pet, and listen to your heart. Do not be afraid of the world. God has a plan for you, and it may not be what you expect. Remember what our Lord said—'Do not fear, for I am with you.'"

His lids fluttered, but with enormous strength of will, Edward kept his eyes open and upon his daughter. "I love you, pet. Remember that."

Vi didn't understand the full meaning of all her father's words, but she knew, just as Ed and Missy did, that he was taking leave of them. If a heart could truly break, hers would have split apart at that moment. There was so much she wanted to say, but where were the words? In all the world, there were no words that could make him well again. He was slipping away before her eyes, and no words could pull him back. Then she saw his mouth move ever so slightly. And she knew he was trying to smile at her. Her throat was choked with pain, but suddenly the words came: "I love you, Papa, and I will never forget. I promise."

Elsie touched each of the three gently, and without wanting to, they stepped back from the bedside as Harold, Herbert, and Rosemary came to take their places. As he had with the eldest, Edward now conveyed a special message of love to each of the younger children.

Last was Danny, held in his mother's arms. Elsie bent forward, holding Danny so that he might give his father a kiss. Even so young, Danny must have sensed the solemn moment, for he kissed and patted Edward's face with heartrending tenderness.

With all his children standing around his bed now, Edward drank in their presence, and a look of peace

seemed to radiate from him. Then he closed his eyes and said in the softest whisper, "You are the sunshine of my days."

Time seemed to stop for them all until Dr. Lansing said, "He is sleeping."

Without being told, the children knew that it was time to leave. Elsie handed Danny to Horace, and Rose took Rosemary's small, trembling hand. Reluctantly but with no hint of protest, the young Travillas left the bedside and were guided from the room by their grandparents and Arthur.

The children begged to remain in the hallway outside the door, but the adults prevailed, and everyone proceeded to the sitting room not far away. Chloe was waiting for them, and she took Danny onto her lap. Molly and Enna were there too, and Molly beckoned to Vi and Missy. Vi took her place next to Enna and was instantly enfolded in her great-aunt's arms. Missy sat beside Molly, and the two young women clasped hands. Horace and Rose retired to a couch, Rose cradling Rosemary and Horace sitting between the twins with one strong arm around each of the boys. Ed took a seat but soon rose and began to pace the floor—his hands clasped behind his back and his handsome head bowed in despondency.

No one spoke. Tears fell from many eyes, but there was no whimpering or sobbing. From the youngest to the eldest, everyone knew that they had entered a time of waiting… and of ending.

# Violet's Hidden Doubts

What was said between Edward and Elsie during that next hour was never fully known. The doctors and the nurse, who tended their patient closely, were too professional to listen and too respectful to reveal what they may have overheard. As for Elsie, though she would tell much, there was more that she would hold in her heart forever. The final words and prayers spoken between husband and wife were for them alone.

The end came near twilight. Edward had fallen into unconsciousness, and Elsie knew without being told that this time, he would not return to her. She sat beside him, holding his hand, and asked Dr. Lansing to summon her family.

They were all with him—wife, children, friends of his lifetime—when Edward Travilla made the journey to his Heavenly home.

Few words were spoken. In a voice strangled with emotion, Dr. Lansing pronounced, "He is gone." And Elsie, still holding the hand of her beloved, quoted softly but clearly Jesus' words from the sixteenth chapter of the book of John: " 'Now is your time of grief, but I will see you again and you will rejoice, and no one will take away your joy…. I came from the Father and entered the world; now I am leaving the world and going back to the Father.' "

In a room grown suddenly dark with sorrow and loss, these words of the Savior shone like a beacon in the storm. Edward Travilla had gone home, to their Heavenly Father, but in time, they would all be reunited. God's promise to His faithful would be fulfilled. Edward was with God now; of that, no one doubted.

For those left behind, the time of grieving had come.

# CHAPTER

8

# Going On

*The LORD is close to the*
*brokenhearted and saves*
*those who are crushed*
*in spirit.*

PSALM 34:18

# Going On

*I*n the days that followed Edward's funeral, Elsie came to wonder how anyone could bear such loss without faith. Elsie had known the depths of sorrow before, and now, in this time of her greatest loss, she turned instinctively to her Savior. In her Bible and through endless hours of prayer, she found solace and understanding. God wanted her to live, and Christ's own life, death, and resurrection showed her the way. She suffered, yet never did her faith waver. Her faith was genuine, and she would go on, with her Lord and Friend always beside her.

❦

As days turned to weeks, Elsie's terrible pain began to give way to hope and determination. She was able to attend to the tasks of mourning—responding to the outpouring of condolences she and the family had received from so many friends near and far. It moved her deeply to read the expressions of others—people of every age and social position—whose lives Edward had touched and bettered in ways that she often had not known about.

Elsie also resumed many of her domestic duties, including daily lessons with the children. At first, going back to the schoolroom seemed awkward for all of them, and they often put aside their assignments simply to talk and pray and sometimes to cry together. Missy and Ed would join them frequently, and most mornings were passed with sweet reminiscences of the man who had been the linchpin of all their lives.

79

# Violet's Hidden Doubts

It was during these times, however, that Elsie began to sense that Vi was not dealing with the loss as might have been expected. Vi would listen to her brothers and sisters with seeming attention. She would sometimes cry with the others, but she rarely participated in their conversations. On those few occasions when she did talk about her papa, it was always some story that did not involve herself. Asked to share a memory, Vi would relate some anecdote about how Edward had helped this person or that person. But Vi's shared memories were impersonal—almost, her mother thought, like newspaper accounts of some event in a distant place.

In the beginning, Elsie credited her daughter's reticence to Vi's innate sensitivity and the normal diffidence of a girl her age. But as time passed and Vi still did not respond, Elsie tried a different approach. She began turning the children back to their schoolwork, hoping that Vi's love of learning might revive her spirits. Elsie continued to talk of Edward with the others, but in a casual way—giving them more individual time outside the schoolroom.

It was not that Vi was difficult. On the contrary, her everyday behavior was almost *too* good. She resumed her studies with diligence. She completed all her chores without complaining. She never squabbled with her siblings—not even when the twins sorely tried her temper with their teasing. And she undertook a new activity that seemed to bode well for her recovery. With her mother's permission, Vi began to accompany Chloe on her daily rounds of the workers' quarters.

"Is she helpful to you?" Elsie asked Chloe about a week after this new routine was initiated.

"A big help," Chloe affirmed. "She carries that heavy basket of medicine for me, and she visits with the old people. You oughta see how she keeps the children entertained, so I can

talk to their mothers. Vi's got a real good way with the little ones, Miss Elsie. They just naturally trust her. But I'll tell you something. I'm worried about our girl."

"How so?" Elsie asked. She had not as yet discussed her own concerns about Vi with anyone else, and she wanted to hear Chloe's observations.

"It's hard to put in words, but she's just not like herself anymore," Chloe said. "She told me the other day that she didn't want any presents for Christmas. When I said that I know how hard it's gonna be this year without Mr. Edward, she said no presents for her ever again. 'I have too much already,' she said. Then she said she don't deserve what she has now—never mind anythin' new. That's not like our Vi. Not that she values presents all that much, but she's always been our Christmas girl and more generous to others than people are to her."

Chloe paused and scratched her head. Then she said, "It's like all the joy just drained outta Vi when Mr. Edward passed. One of the little boys was cuttin' up down at the quarters today, being funny, and I saw Vi smiling at him. But as soon as the child went his way, Vi's smile just vanished. Just vanished, Miss Elsie, quick as a wink. I thought to myself that she's not lettin' herself have even that little pleasure. It's like she's punishin' herself for somethin'."

Elsie agreed with Chloe that Vi was acting oddly and then confided her own worries to her old nursemaid.

"Have you tried to talk to her?" Chloe asked.

"I have," Elsie said, "and I cannot complain of her responses. She is polite and she answers my questions honestly. But she is not—" Elsie paused, trying to find the right word. "She isn't *forthcoming*. Our old Vi could sometimes keep her feelings to herself, but I never knew her to hold back like this."

# Violet's Hidden Doubts

"You're right that she's never been one to keep her secrets for long," Chloe concurred. "But Mr. Edward's dying, it's taken a toll on all the children. I'd be wrong to expect each of them to act just alike. Maybe Vi just needs more time than the others to begin the healin'. But I'm gonna keep my eye on her all the same."

"Please do," Elsie said. "Something is troubling her, Chloe, but I hardly know how to help her. I have an idea that she is carrying a burden that goes beyond the loss of her father; yet how can I help if I don't know what it is?"

Elsie knew from sad experience that grief is easier to bear when shared. And whenever her own pain threatened to overwhelm her, she turned to her parents. To Horace and Rose, Elsie could unhesitatingly confide her fears—that she was insufficient to be both mother and father to her children, that she did not have the skills to take Edward's place as the head of Ion, that she lacked the strength to support those who now depended on her alone.

So Elsie naturally sought out her father and stepmother and told them what Chloe had said. They, too, had noticed signs of change in Vi.

Rose asked a difficult question that Elsie had also pondered: "Do you think Vi is suffering from some crisis of faith? I mean, is it possible that she may be having doubts that Edward is in a better place? She is of a vulnerable age, and Edward's death was so sudden and unexpected."

Elsie said, "I have considered that, but I do not think so. When I can get her to talk of Edward, she seems sincerely to believe that he is with our Heavenly Father now. No, I

do not believe that her faith has been shaken. In fact, I think her trust in God is the one comfort she allows herself. It is something else."

"Perhaps she needs more time," Horace suggested.

"That's what Chloe says," Elsie relied. "And you are probably right. If only Edward were here," she added wistfully. "He would know what to do."

One evening a few days before Christmas, Vi and the older children retired to the parlor with Elsie, Rose, and Horace after supper. Missy sat at the piano and began to play. She chose a rustic tune that had been a favorite of her father's, and soon Ed and the twins were blending their voices in the familiar song. When they finished, Elsie asked for another song, naming one that had been popular when she and Edward were newlyweds. The young Travillas were not sure of the words, so Elsie, Horace, and Rose taught them a verse and then led them through the chorus.

The songs seemed to open the floodgates of memory, and Horace related to his grandchildren the tale of an amusing adventure that he and Edward had had when they were young men traveling in Europe. It was a story the children had not heard before, and they asked their grandpapa for more tales of their father's youth. Horace happily obliged, and the parlor was soon ringing with the sounds of laughter and happy conversation.

The evening wore on, and no one noticed the passage of time until Elsie saw that Harold's eyelids were growing heavy and Herbert was stifling a yawn.

# Violet's Hidden Doubts

"Oh, my dears," she said, "the clock is about to strike ten, and it is time to prepare for bed. It has been so pleasant an evening, but I must bring it to an end."

"It has been pleasant, Mamma," Missy agreed.

"The kind of night Papa always enjoyed," Ed added.

Horace happened to be looking at Vi, and he saw a dark look pass over her face. Sensing that she and the others were surprised by their good moods, he said, "I feel sure that your father would be happy tonight to hear music and laughter in this house once more."

"But is it right of us?" Vi burst out. "How can we enjoy ourselves when Papa is not here!"

Elsie reached out to Vi and drew her close. "Your Papa is *here*," she said, laying her hand over Vi's heart. "His memory lives in all our hearts. We have shed tears for him, but our laughter honors him as well, for there was never a man who took more delight in the laughter of his children. Trust me, dearest. When we find joy in our memories of the times we had with Papa, we are honoring him more than any monument carved of the finest marble in the world ever could."

"If he were standing right here, I bet he'd be making a joke with us right now," Harold said.

"And then chasing us up to bed," Herbert added.

Vi still looked doubtful, but Ed teased her gently. "Smile for us, little sister, for when you smile, you look just like Papa. Your eyes sparkle, and you get that little dimple at the corner of your mouth."

"What dimple?" Vi asked in amazement.

"Do you not know?" Missy replied. "Why, Violet, you have always been the image of Papa. If you smile at yourself in the mirror, you'll see it. And you are the only one of us who has it. It's Papa's special legacy to you."

# Going On

This statement was a kind of revelation for Vi, and quite beyond her control, her face brightened.

"There it is," Ed exclaimed jovially, "the famous Travilla dimple!"

"Good!" said Harold in a rush of relief. "Vi's smiling, and I'm awfully sleepy."

"May we be excused, Mamma?" Herbert asked for himself and his brother.

"Of course, boys," Elsie said, keeping Vi at her side. "Go up now, and I will join you soon for prayers."

As the twins bounded from the room, Ed and Missy were bidding good night to their grandparents. Vi looked into her mother's face and said in a whisper, "I'm sorry if I said something wrong, Mamma. I don't want to make you sad."

"You didn't say anything wrong, Vi darling," Elsie said reassuringly. "Not at all. I do not expect you to keep your feelings hidden. I would be sad if I thought you could not express yourself within your family. Come, now, and let us say good night to Grandmamma and Grandpapa. Then I'll accompany you upstairs, and perhaps we may talk a bit more, if you like."

Later, in her room, Vi did open her heart a little way to her mother. For the first time since Edward's death, Vi shared some of her personal memories of him.

"Do you remember when I got lost in the middle of the night and Papa found me?" Vi asked.

"I remember all too well," Elsie said. "You were sleepwalking, and somehow you got out through a parlor window and wandered all the way down the drive to the road. When Missy found your bed empty, she raised the alarm, and everyone began searching high and low. Your father found a torn piece of your nightgown on the window, and he followed your

trail until he finally found you huddled under a tree not far from the road."

"I don't remember much," Vi said softly, "except that I was very scared and I thought I saw monsters."

"They weren't monsters," Elsie said, "but you did see something awful. We didn't realize until later that you had witnessed a brutal attack by several Ku Klux Klan members on one of our neighbors."

Vi lay her head against her mother's shoulder and said softly, "I do remember praying for Jesus to let Papa find me, and He did. And I remember feeling safe because Papa was carrying me and telling me that there are no monsters. I've always wondered how Papa knew where to look for me."

"Perhaps he knew because he had also been a sleepwalker when he was a child," Elsie replied, "and he once became lost just as you did. You and your Papa share so many qualities, and sleepwalking was just one of them. I am very thankful that you both outgrew it."

"Me too," Vi said with a deep yawn.

"It's time for you to sleep, dearest," Elsie said. She kissed her daughter's forehead and bade her good night. When she left Vi's room, Elsie thought to herself that something important had just happened—that this sharing of memories might be the beginning of a breakthrough.

With a hopeful heart, Elsie silently prayed: *Dear Heavenly Father, thank You for giving me this glimpse into my child's true heart. Bless her, dear Lord, with the healing grace of Your endless love. Please guide me, as You always guided Edward, to calm Vi's fears and help her through her time of grief and sadness.*

# CHAPTER

## 9

# A Brother's Departure

*If we confess our sins, he is faithful
and just and will forgive us our
sins and purify us from
all unrighteousness.*

1 JOHN 1:9

# A Brother's Departure

*W*inter turned unusually cold and bitter that year, and it seemed to Vi that even nature was grieving the loss of one who had always greeted each new season in the spirit of hope and renewal. There were several heavy snows in December and January, but without her father, Vi found no joy in the fluffy blankets of white that cloaked the hard ground and enticed the younger children out to play. She had a new worry on her mind.

Ed would soon be leaving for the University, and she could hardly bear to think of Ion without him. She knew that he must go—that he would honor his promise to his father so that he could someday take over the running of Ion. She didn't want to hold her brother back, for their father's wish was Ed's as well. But just the thought of being separated from her beloved big brother sent chills through her that had nothing to do with snow and ice.

She often thought about unburdening herself to Ed and telling him the truth of what she'd done. He would understand better than anyone, she was sure. But each time she started to speak, something held her back. She would tell herself that it was not the right time, that she would talk to him another day. But the days passed, and still she guarded her secret.

Then the days dwindled to hours, and Ed would be leaving the next morning. One last time, Vi would try to find the words to unlock her troubled heart.

# Violet's Hidden Doubts

Ed was tucking the last of his traveling clothes into his case when he heard a knock at his bedroom door. "Come in," he called and looked up to see Vi enter.

"Here to bid your big brother a fond farewell?" he asked playfully as he went back to his packing.

But Vi didn't reply. She walked to Ed's bookcase, now half-empty because his favorite volumes and his other things had already been shipped ahead. She ran her fingers along the spines of the books that remained—mostly adventure tales that he had loved when he was a boy.

Wondering what was on her mind, Ed said, "You can have those if you like, Vi. They're ripping good stories."

"I've read most of them," she said in a flat tone.

"Well, I haven't much else to give you, little sister, unless you'd like a piece of my mind before I go," he joked.

Vi, who had always been quick to answer her brother's jesting with her own, said nothing, and Ed let the matter go. *She has something on her mind*, he thought. *Give her time. That's what Papa would do.*

Several minutes passed, and Ed was about to close his case when Vi said, "Don't forget your Bible. It's on your table."

Ed hadn't forgotten; he planned to pack the Bible in his small valise so it would be at hand on his journey. But he said only, "Thanks, Vi. I'll remember."

She had turned her back, appearing to look at the books again, when she said, "Do you remember your accident, Ed? When you were little and you—ah—hurt Papa?"

"As clear as yesterday," he replied evenly.

"What did you do when it happened? I mean, did you tell what you had done?"

Ed was staring at her back now. He had no idea why she was asking him these questions, but he knew that she had no desire to cause him pain, so he answered as truthfully as he could. "No, I didn't tell at first. After the gun went off and I knew that Papa was injured, I just fell on the ground crying, and poor Archie Leland stayed with me. We were in that little grove down by the bend in the driveway. No one could see us, and no one knew that I had done the shooting. I guess I knew that I had to tell, but I was so stunned with guilt and fear for Papa that I couldn't move. It was Crystal who found us there, a long time later as I remember it. It wasn't till the next morning that I was able to see Papa and confess that I'd fired the shot that wounded him."

"Did you feel better…after you confessed?"

"Yes, in a way. I never planned to lie. And Papa forgave me immediately. I was punished, of course, but not harshly. I asked God to forgive me, and I knew that He did. But do you know the worst part, Vi?"

She turned now and looked at him at last.

Seeing the anxiety in her face, he said, "The worst part was forgiving myself. I wasn't even eight years old, yet I knew that I had almost caused the death of one of the two people I loved most in all the world. And I knew that if I had killed Papa, that it would almost be like killing Mamma as well. But why do you want to know about all that?"

Vi kept her gaze steadily on him as she said, "Because I was too little to realize what was going on, and I've never asked how you felt. And you're leaving tomorrow morning, and I just thought I should know. I mean, Missy says that what happened changed you, and I just wanted to know…" She hesitated, unsure how to say what was in her heart.

Sensing her uncertainty, Ed smiled and motioned to her to come and sit beside him on the bed.

"I hope it changed me for the better," he said. "As young as I was, I knew that the whole thing was my fault; it was my hotheadedness and my pride. My cousins had that gun, and they were teasing me, saying that I was a baby because I wouldn't touch it. I let them get my goat, and I did something I knew not to do. Even as I grabbed the gun and pulled the trigger, I knew it was wrong. Papa helped me so much, Vi. He didn't make excuses for me like some parents do, but he didn't blame me either. I guess he understood that my conscience was punishing me more than he ever could. But he talked with me a lot, and he helped me begin to understand what it means to be responsible."

"What did Papa say it means?" she asked.

"Well, that being responsible means taking the blame when we do something wrong. But it also means thinking before we do something that might be wrong and considering the possible results of our actions."

She looked at him. "But what if you did something that most people wouldn't think was wrong. What if you didn't even know if what you did was really wrong?"

He gazed at her earnest face for several moments before he said, "Do you mean something that troubles your own heart even though it might not trouble others?"

She nodded.

He thought again and then said, "I'd talk to our Lord. When I feel guilty about anything, I take it to Him and ask Him to forgive me and to wash me clean again. And then I try to make amends as best I can. If I think I've wronged someone, I talk to the person and tell him what I did."

Vi dropped her eyes and said softly, "But we can't always make amends, Ed. We just can't."

Very gently he asked, "Won't you tell me what's troubling you, Vi? I'm nowhere near as good at this as Papa, but I'm a pretty good listener."

She shrugged and forced a smile as she replied, "I'm fine, really I am. It's just that you're leaving and Papa is gone, and I'm going to miss you so much!"

Tears suddenly streamed from her eyes, and Ed quickly put his arm around her shoulders to comfort her. "Not half as much as I'll miss you," he said. "If there's something bothering you and you can't figure it out for yourself, promise me that you will talk to Mamma or Grandpapa or Grandmamma. Will you do that for me, pretty Violet?"

When she didn't answer, he lightened his tone and joked, "If you try to keep everything inside, you'll pop, and that would not be pretty at all."

Vi looked into his face. Though her cheeks were wet with tears, she smiled, and Ed saw the dimple appear. He took that as her answer.

The next morning was cold but clear—one of those early February mornings when the hard and frost-covered ground twinkles like a carpet of diamonds in the sun. Some tears were shed as Ed prepared to leave, but there was also much cheerful jesting as his family bade him Godspeed. Horace reminded him to telegraph home as soon as he reached his destination. Crystal and Chloe made sure he had the package of sandwiches and cakes they'd prepared, and Ben checked the carriage one last

time, assuring himself that there were blankets inside to warm Ed's journey.

Bundled against the cold, the family stood around the carriage, and everyone had one last good wish to bestow upon Ed, one final hug and hearty handshake. Ed paid special attention to Vi, but she seemed to be all right again — a little withdrawn, but that had been her way of late. When he hugged her, she whispered, "Thanks for the advice, Eddie. I'm very glad you're my big brother."

Teasingly, he responded, "That's *Ed*, little sister, and don't you forget it."

No one wanted to let him go, but Elsie stepped forward, took her son's arm, and turned him to the open carriage door. She kissed his cheek and said, "The Spanish have an expression, 'Vaya con Dios.' It means, 'Go with God.' I will miss you, my darling, but I know that God is your constant companion and watches over you always. Now go, Ed, with my love. The world is waiting for you."

He stepped up into the carriage, and Elsie signaled to the driver. The horses pulled away; the carriage rolled down the drive, picking up speed, and was soon out of sight. The others quickly sought the warmth of the house, but Vi still stood in the drive, her eyes on the bend in the road where the carriage had turned and disappeared from view. She hardly noticed the cold and might have remained standing there for a long time. But her mother called her inside, and Vi put her lonely thoughts into hiding — as she was now in the habit of doing. She went into the house to begin another day of pretending to be happy.

# CHAPTER

# 10

# Searching for Answers

*I sought the LORD, and he answered me; he delivered me from all my fears.*

PSALM 34:4

*E*d had been at school for six weeks, and from poring over his letters home, everyone could tell that he'd made the correct choice. Horace and Rose had returned to The Oaks, though Horace managed to find some reason to ride to Ion almost every day. And the Travillas were not without other company. Isa Conley, their cousin who was now twenty-one, appeared almost as often as Horace, sometimes bringing her older sister, Virginia. Cal and Arthur Conley came whenever their busy schedules permitted. Other friends and relatives stopped by, and their company proved to be of great solace to Elsie and the children.

The Travillas also made the short trip to Roselands at least twice each week, for old Mr. Horace Dinsmore, Sr. — Elsie's grandfather — was mostly housebound. Edward Travilla had been much more than a grandson-in-law to the elderly head of the Dinsmore family. He had been a close friend, and the senior Mr. Dinsmore felt the loss keenly. But the frequent visits of his granddaughter and great-grandchildren never failed to lift his spirits. Even his daughter Louise Conley, who cared for her father at Roselands, allowed her frosty façade to slip a bit when Elsie came to call. Louise, embittered by the death of her husband in the War, had never hidden her jealousy of Elsie's happiness. But perhaps now that Elsie, too, was a widow, Louise sensed the bond that they shared.

As the first signs of the season's turning appeared — the bright yellows of forsythia and crocuses and early daffodils that always foretold the return of the warming sunlight of

spring—Elsie felt a growing confidence in her ability to guide Ion and its operations.

"Edward would be most pleased with the way you are managing, my dear," Horace said one morning as he and Elsie enjoyed coffee together before going about their separate tasks.

"Do you really think so, Papa?" Elsie asked. "I feel his absence so acutely at times, especially when a major decision must be made."

"And what decision do you face today?" he inquired.

"I received word from Viamede some days ago that our plantation manager, Mr. Spriggs, wishes to leave his post as soon as I can find a replacement. In the same letter, he informed me that Dr. Bayliss, who has for so long tended to the health of our workers, is planning to retire. But worst of all is the news that came yesterday. Our dear chaplain, Mr. Mason, writes that he has been offered a teaching position at a seminary in St. Louis. He says that he will gladly stay with his congregations if no replacement can be found. But I can tell that this appointment means the world to him, and I would do nothing to hold him back.

"With so many changes at once, I think I should go to Louisiana. Yet how can I leave the children, Papa? This just is not the right time for me to be away. The loss of their father is still so fresh, and Ed is no longer at home. I don't think they need another separation, especially when I may be required at Viamede for two months or more."

"I agree," Horace said thoughtfully. "This is not the time for a lengthy separation. Yet with such important jobs falling vacant at Viamede, you are needed there as well. I could go in your place, but it's important that you make such hiring decisions."

"I thought of taking the entire family," Elsie remarked tentatively.

"And what do you think Edward would have said to that idea?" Horace asked.

Elsie smiled. "You know exactly what he would say. 'Pack them up, Elsie my dear. Pack each in a trunk—a valise will do for Danny—and ship them off on the next steamer to New Orleans.'"

Horace laughed at her imitation. "I can almost hear him speaking those very words."

Suddenly Horace slapped his knee and jumped up from his chair with the spring of a boy of sixteen. "He would be right, too!" he declared. "Let's pack up and go to Viamede. Your mother and I would be delighted to accompany you. And Molly, of course. And Enna and her nurse. And Christine for the little ones."

"It seems there will be no one left at Ion," Elsie said, laughing as she caught her father's enthusiasm. He was pacing the room now, and Elsie saw something very like a little hop in his step.

"Ion will be perfectly safe in the competent hands of your manager and Ben and Crystal," he said.

"And Aunt Chloe and Joe," Elsie added, "though I shall miss their company."

"I know," Horace said, his face clouding for a moment, "but Joe cannot make a long trip, and Chloe would never leave him behind. Still," he brightened, "it will be good for the rest of us. We can leave in two weeks and miss the worst of the fever season. I shall book our boat passages this very day. Oh, my dear, I fully expect this visit to bring the apples back to all my grandchildren's cheeks— Vi particularly."

# Violet's Hidden Doubts

"I thought she was improving," Elsie sighed, "but now I'm not sure."

"Vi is still trying very hard not to show her sorrow," Horace observed, "but she does seem to be taking more interest in activities."

Elsie shook her head and said, "I cannot explain myself well, but I still see signs of some hidden doubt or fear or guilt—whatever it is. I don't think I'm being overly protective, Papa. Something weighs on our Violet, and she cannot go on like this, bearing it alone." Her voice broke as she said, "If she would only share it with me, I know that I could help her."

"She will," Horace said gently, "when she's ready. Our Heavenly Friend is her comfort and guide, and He will lead her to you in time. Her path may be arduous, but He will not let her fall. We must trust Him and have faith in His ways."

Then he added, "Perhaps this trip will do her good. A change of scene may be what Vi needs. At Viamede, she may begin to see things differently."

So it was decided, and everyone was soon engaged in preparations for their journey to Viamede—the Louisiana bayou plantation where Elsie had been born. It was at Viamede that Elsie always felt closest to the mother she had never known.

When she'd told her children about the plans, they'd all been excited, and even Vi seemed to look forward to the trip. Maybe Horace was right, and what Vi needed was a change of scene.

As the day of their departure approached, Elsie was often engaged with business matters, so Missy and Chloe supervised the packing. "Our Miss Rosemary got herself in a twist yesterday when we said she couldn't take a whole trunk load of her dolls and toys," Chloe chuckled one day as she made her progress report to Elsie.

"Oh, dear," Elsie said, "I hope she didn't have a temper tantrum."

"Well, Miss Elsie, she's got Dinsmore blood in her veins, and she can be mulish like her grandpa and great-grandpa," Chloe replied with a grin. "But when I told her about all those toys in the nursery down at Viamede and how they were the things you played with and her Grandmother Elsie, too—well, she calmed down right quick."

Elsie relaxed. "I can always trust you to find a solution, Chloe," she said. "I will miss you terribly while we're away."

"You know I'm gonna be missing you and the children every minute," Chloe said, the smile fading from her still handsome face. "I'd have liked to visit Dinah and her family down in New Orleans, but I'll get there in God's good time."

"You must be so proud of Dinah and Reverend Carpenter and their new mission," Elsie replied, referring to the New Orleans ministry founded by Chloe's granddaughter and her husband. "I just wish Dinah could continue teaching. She is so gifted."

"But she has," Chloe said. "Dinah's got herself a school started right there in the mission, doin' God's work by teaching readin' and writin' to every poor child who walks through her door. You think you might see Dinah while you're down in Louisiana?"

"Yes, I will," Elsie said. "I certainly will."

"Then you give her and my great-grandbabies lots of hugs and kisses from their Chloe and Joe."

"I will," Elsie promised. Then another thought struck her. "Perhaps it will do Vi good to see Dinah and visit the mission," she mused almost to herself.

"That's a fine idea," Chloe said. "Just fine. It just might do our Vi a world of good. Somethin' different might be what she needs to get out of them doldrums."

"Mamma, have you seen Vi anywhere?" Missy asked. It was the afternoon of the day before the family would leave for Viamede.

"No, dear, but she will turn up," Elsie answered.

"I want to tell her about Cousin Isa coming with us now that Aunt Louise has finally given her permission. But I have been searching for an hour, and Vi is nowhere to be found."

"Did you try the kitchen?"

"I did."

"Molly's room?"

"Molly hasn't seen her since breakfast. I even went down to the stables."

Elsie thought for a moment then said, "The lake. You know how she loves to sketch in the afternoon light."

"Of course," Missy sighed. "Where is my head? I should have looked there first."

"I imagine that at least a part of your mind lingers on a certain handsome artist on foreign shores, my dear, and not the banks of our little lake," Elsie said with a smile. "When you find your sister, tell her to come in now, for twilight is approaching."

After brushing her mother's cheek with a quick kiss, Missy hurried from the sitting room, and Elsie returned her full attention to some important correspondence she was completing.

Some twenty minutes passed before Missy returned—without Vi.

"She was not at her favorite place by the lake, and there's no sign of her drawing things," Missy said breathlessly. "I looked all around the lake, and I checked upstairs again, too. Mamma, I'm getting worried. Where can she be?"

Missy's words and anxious expression caused a prickling sensation to lift the hairs on the back of Elsie's neck, but smiling, she rose from her little desk and went to Missy, taking her hand.

"Don't fret now, darling. In your diligent search, you have probably crossed paths with her unknowingly—you going up the front stairs while she came down the back way. I'm finished with my letters and could do with some exercise. I will take up the search while you help Christine with the little ones."

Elsie looked down at the little watch pinned to her blouse. "My goodness," she said. "Supper will be ready in less than an hour. You run along and see that everyone is neat and tidy. And remind the twins to wash behind their ears."

Her mother's casual air reassured Missy, and she left to find her brothers. But Elsie was not as lighthearted as she appeared. It wasn't like Vi to disappear and tell no one where she would be.

*Do not panic*, she told herself. *Vi is here, and you will find her. Now, think. Where might she go? She probably wanted to be alone, and she usually goes to the lake when she is in a solitary mood. But I can depend on Missy to have made a thorough search there.*

# Violet's Hidden Doubts

From deep in Elsie's memory, a small idea began to emerge, like a shadowy form seen through a fog. Her brow furrowed as she struggled to lift the haze. *Concentrate!* she commanded herself. *Oh, Lord, help me remember!*

And there it was—a picture clear in every detail. But was it the right picture?

Elsie dashed from the library to the back stairs of the house. Gathering her skirts about her like a little girl at play, she climbed the steps. At the rear of the house was a kind of half-floor, some four feet above the second floor, where two uninhabited rooms and the entrance to the attic were located. Elsie went up the short flight of wooden steps, but at the landing, she paused. Taking deep breaths, she calmed her rapidly beating heart and relaxed her shoulders. Quietly, she walked to the door at the right side of the narrow, roughly plastered hallway and carefully turned the knob. *Dear Jesus, I felt You guide me here. Please let me be right.*

"Violet?" she asked of the still, damply chill air in the luggage room. Light, what little there was of it, came from a small oil lamp on the floor in one far corner. "Are you here, pet? Are you all right?"

"Yes, Mamma," came a faint voice from the opposite corner of the room. "I'm here."

# CHAPTER

**11**

# Released from Darkness

*Then your light will break forth
like the dawn, and your healing
will quickly appear....*

ISAIAH 58:8

e've been looking for you," Elsie said as she approached a pile of old trunks atop the largest of which her daughter was sitting. "Missy has been searching high and low. She wanted to tell you that Cousin Isa will be traveling to Viamede with us."

"That's very nice, Mamma," Vi replied flatly. "I've just been here. I went to the cemetery first, to Papa's grave. Then I came up here."

Elsie drew near and sat down on the lowest trunk in the stack. Her instinct had been to put her arms around her child and lead her by the hand from this stuffy, cold room back to the warmth of the family. But a voice seemed to speak deep inside her, saying, *Not yet*.

"It took me some time to remember this place," Elsie said, trying to keep her voice even. "You used to play here by yourself. Your father would say that this was your 'special place,' but I'd almost forgotten about it." Then without skipping a beat, she added, "What were you thinking about when I came in?"

"Papa. I was…" Vi stopped herself, for she had almost said something she intended to keep to herself.

"Ah," Elsie sighed. She was going to ask another question, but the inner voice that was guiding her said, *Be silent, and wait*.

There was no clock in the room to tick away the minutes. To Elsie it seemed that a very long time passed before Vi finally said in that strange, flat tone, "I was trying to talk to Papa. It's silly, but I just thought that if I was here, he might

hear me. I wanted—I want—I have to tell him that I'm sorry."

With enormous self-control, Elsie remained silent. She had no idea what Vi wanted to say, and she could not risk putting the wrong words in her daughter's mouth. Then she heard a little noise almost, she thought, like a baby's burp. The noise was repeated and magnified—not a burp but a sob.

Then came a gasp of pure anguish as Vi cried, "I can't hold it inside any longer, and it won't go away!"

There was another wrenching gasp as Vi at last released the secret she had been struggling for so long to bury: "It's my fault he's dead, Mamma! It was my fault, and I can't ask him to forgive me! He's dead because of me, Mamma, and sometimes I wish I were dead with him!"

A thundering of sobs echoed in the small room, and Elsie's instincts took over. She leapt up, grabbed Vi, and pulled the girl from the high trunk and into her embrace. She held Vi as tightly as if they both were caught in a buffeting storm, cradling the girl's head against her shoulder.

The sobbing shook Vi's thin body with such force that Elsie began to fear her child was suffering a seizure of some sort. But she did not release her hold, and after some terrifying minutes, the sobs and shaking seemed to lessen in intensity. Still Elsie held Vi, and at last she spoke in a soft, crooning manner.

"You did not kill your father. You did not. It was an accident caused by no one. It was an accident like Enna's accident when she fell into the lake. You did nothing to harm your Papa. You must believe that."

Vi's sobbing gradually subsided into little, wet hiccups, and through her tears, she managed to say, "But I could

108

have stopped him that day. If I hadn't been so—so—so self-ish, he wouldn't have been in the field. He'd be alive right now, but for me."

"Why do you think that, dearest child?" Elsie asked.

"Because he wanted me to go with him and have a pic-nic," Vi replied, "and I said"—she gulped for air—"I said 'no' because I wanted to show off my French to you. If I'd gone with him, I know that he wouldn't have been cutting that tree. He'd have been with me. We might have ridden somewhere together, and he wouldn't have been anywhere near that tree when it fell. But I just thought about myself and my perfect French lesson. And I'd spoken so rudely to him at breakfast."

"But he had forgiven you for that," Elsie said, caressing Vi's hair. "He told me so. He told me that he had asked your forgiveness as well."

"He told you?"

"Just before he left the house that morning. He said that you two had made your plans for the next day, and that he was very proud of you for being responsible and tending to your studies."

"He did?"

"I would not tell you a falsehood," Elsie said. "And I can tell you that you could not have prevented the accident had you been standing at his side. Your father wanted to work with the men that day. He looked forward to the work. And he was struck because he stood his ground until all the men were out of danger. Ben has told us everything that hap-pened. When your father ran, he became entangled in the undergrowth and could not reach safety. Do you hold your-self responsible for the falling of the tree or the twisting of the vines?"

# Violet's Hidden Doubts

Hesitantly, Vi answered, "N—no, Mamma. But I remember the story about the time when Papa and Grandpapa were boys, and Grandpapa was nearly shot by one of their friends. That was an accident, but Papa always said he was as guilty as if he'd fired the rifle himself. And I talked to Ed about what he did to Papa. That was an accident, too, but Ed was responsible because he could have prevented it. But they were able to ask forgiveness and make amends. I can't do that, Mamma, because Papa is gone," she sighed.

"Your father felt guilty because he had allowed others to be careless. Ed was responsible because he let his temper get the best of him. It is not the same. Papa's accident was not caused by carelessness or thoughtlessness—neither yours nor anyone else's."

Elsie finally released her grip on her daughter. She seated the girl on the low trunk and then fetched the oil lamp from the far corner of the room and placed it nearby. Sitting down, Elsie drew Vi to her and said gently, "You've been carrying a heavy burden of guilt, my child, but it is time to lay it down. Think now. When you decided not to go with your father that day, did you act from anger or the desire to hurt him in some way? Did you know that he was in danger yet do nothing to prevent it?"

Vi looked into her mother's eyes, and even in the pale light, Elsie could read the shock in her daughter's face. "Oh, no, Mamma!" Vi exclaimed. "I really wanted to go with him. But I wanted more to recite my lesson to you. I'd worked very hard on it, and I was afraid I might forget the passage if I put it off. I just thought Papa would be there the next day, and we'd have our picnic and ride then. But he wasn't there, and he never will be there again!"

"Am I responsible because I didn't ask him to stay at the house that day?"

"Never, Mamma! You couldn't have known."

"Nor could you," Elsie said with some firmness. She slid her arm around Vi and drew her closer. "Don't you see, darling, that we cannot take responsibility for what might have been? Remember what is said in Proverbs: 'Do not boast about tomorrow, for you do not know what a day may bring forth.' Only God knows what each day, or even the smallest part of the next second, may bring. We're responsible for our actions and must carefully consider the possible consequences of what we do, but God does not expect us to see into the future or feel guilt for that which is beyond our power to control.

"Consider this, too. When your father asked you to accompany him to the field that day, he offered you—from his own free will—a choice, and he respected your decision. It was very important to him that you and your brothers and sisters learn to make good choices and to feel confident in your decisions. That day you chose—for reasons your father approved wholeheartedly—to stay at home and attend to your lessons. He chose to go to the fields and work. There is no more guilt attached to your choice than to your Papa's."

Vi sniffled and then said, "I never thought of that, Mamma. Papa's dying was so horrible, and I miss him so much. It hurts worse than anything I've ever felt—even worse than when Lily died."

"And you wanted to blame someone for your pain, so you blamed yourself," Elsie said. "We humans tend to do that when we cannot understand the reasons for our suffering. But there is much that we are not meant to understand—

things beyond our comprehension. God alone has infinite knowledge and wisdom, and He wants us to open our hearts and trust in Him even when we are suffering."

"The lesson of Job?" Vi said.

"Yes, dearest child. Suffering is part of God's great plan for us—as is joy. It's not for us to question His reasons but to trust that He does what is right for us. Never forget or doubt that God is in control and is working out His perfect plan in the lives of all His children. Hold fast to the truth that God is good and all He does is good."

Elsie paused to allow her words to sink in. Then she continued. "As we choose to trust Him, we will find moment by moment the help and strength we need. The Bible promises that 'the Lord is close to the brokenhearted.' He will never fail you, Vi. And what's more, He gives us the comfort of one another." She hugged Vi affectionately, and then said, "I am glad you have confided in me, darling, though I wish we had spoken of this earlier. Have you taken all your feelings to Jesus? Have you poured out your heart to Him?"

"Yes, Mamma, but I think that I wasn't truly listening for His answer," Vi replied, shaking her head from side to side as if she were trying to dislodge some thought.

"Ever since Papa died, I've felt like I've been going around in a circle. I pray, and I feel so much better. Then I start thinking about what happened, and I come right back to the beginning—to feeling so guilty and so terribly sad. I thought if I punished myself, that would make the feelings go away. But no matter what I did, they just came back, worse than ever...."

Vi paused, and Elsie knew that her child needed to gather her thoughts. After a minute or two, Vi resumed: "I'm beginning to see that I've been too deep in my own

sadness. It's as if I've been locked away in one of these dusty old trunks with nothing but my guilty feelings all around me. God has been answering my prayers all along, but my ears and eyes have been closed to everything but my sorrow."

"God was answering my prayers, wasn't He?" said Vi, and her voice was lighter than Elsie had heard in many months. "He gave me you and everyone who loves me and wants to listen to me. Only I couldn't see that He wanted me to tell you how I felt."

Then Vi flung her arms about her mother and exclaimed, "I'm so happy that our Lord led you to find me here, Mamma. I know He helped you remember this place because He's been watching over me all along and He directed you to come to me. Don't you think that, Mamma? Don't you think that the Lord is truly the greatest and most loving Friend?"

"I do, darling," Elsie said from the bottom of her heart. "I do."

"Mamma," Vi said, her tone serious once again, "does it seem to you that I am very different from your other children? I never seem to feel things the way Missy and Ed and the rest do. I've wanted so much to be like them — to be sad but also glad for Papa, that he's with God now. But I just kept thinking how disappointed God must be by my selfishness. I thought He couldn't forgive me and Papa couldn't forgive me. And you, Mamma — how could I make your suffering worse by telling you my feelings?"

Gently, Elsie said, "There is much of your father in you, you know. But I see myself there, too. When I was a girl, I often tried to hold my feelings inside, lest I cause pain to those I loved. I didn't understand that keeping fear and

doubt hidden in the dark gives them the power to torment us. But I learned through trial and error—and with much help from your Papa—that the Lord wants us to bring our feelings into the light and share our troubles with those who care about us. God doesn't want us to suffer alone, and His abiding love for us includes the gift of other people to help us in our misery and grief."

"I wanted to tell you, Mamma, so many times. I wanted to tell Ed before he left. But whenever I tried, I couldn't get the words out of my mouth. I was so ashamed," Vi said, her voice trembling as she recalled her terrible loneliness over the last months. "I was so confused and frightened."

"I know that, pet," Elsie said. "But even when we think that our worries are completely hidden, the people who really love us can sense our feelings. They might not know the cause of our sorrow, but nonetheless our pain is painful for them."

"Did you know?" Vi asked.

"I knew that you were suffering, and I grieved at your grief," Elsie answered honestly. "I knew that I would do anything in my power to help you, if you would let me."

Elsie hugged her daughter gently and said, "I trust your good and loving heart and the healing power of the Lord. But I have worried a great deal about you. I wanted to help, Vi, and now you have allowed me to. That makes me feel very good. From the time you were a small girl, you were always able to turn to your Papa when you were troubled. I can never take his place, but I am here for you, my darling. No one can protect you from all the troubles of life, but believe me, Vi, troubles are easier to bear when they are shared."

"Would it be all right…" Vi began. Then she hesitated. After a moment, she resumed, "Would it be all right to keep

this between us, Mamma? I mean, should I share what I told you with the others?"

"Only if you want to," Elsie replied. "What is most important for you is to learn the lesson of opening yourself completely to our Heavenly Father and holding nothing back from Him. I know that it's hard for you, because you think you are imposing your troubles on Him. But that is what the Lord wants—to share our troubles and to bear them for us. The Bible says, 'Cast all your anxiety on him because he cares for you.' And the Lord also gives us people who love us to help us through our pain. When we allow ourselves to be helped, then we are better able to help others in their times of need."

Vi smiled, and Elsie continued. "You said that you felt as if you were going around in a circle, and I understand now that you must have been very frightened because you thought that you were in that circle alone and you could not see your way out. But God was with you all the time, and He always will be. That is what it means to open our hearts to Him. When we invite Him into our hearts, then we are never alone. Instead of a circle of pain, His is a circle of love—love that is without beginning and without end."

In the near-dark of that small, cold room, Vi leaned against her mother and felt the love—pure and warm—surrounding her. For the first time in so many months, she was free of the shadows of her guilt and regret.

Softly, she said, "That is what everyone has been trying to tell me—Molly and Ed and you, Mamma, and God most of all. And now I can hear you. Oh, thank You, God, for answering my prayers by bringing my Mamma here to me tonight."

Elsie added her own words: "Yes, thank You, Heavenly Father, for bringing us together and showing us Your way."

And for some minutes, mother and daughter simply sat together, embracing each other and warming themselves in the embrace of the greatest love of all.

But at last Elsie became aware of the time, and she said, "I want to talk more of this with you, for I believe we both have many lessons to learn together. For the moment, however, I think our family will best be served by our appearance in the dining room. They are surely wondering where we are. Are you hungry, my pet?"

The wick in the lamp had burned so low that Elsie couldn't see her daughter's face, but she heard the amazement in Vi's response.

"I am, Mamma. I don't know why, for I have hardly wanted to eat anything lately. But all of a sudden, I'm starving! Isn't that strange, Mamma?"

And Elsie could not control the smile that came to her lips on hearing those words. *Thank You, dear Lord*, she thought, *for bringing Vi home to us again*!

"I'm strangely hungry myself," Elsie said as she took her daughter's hand and they departed the luggage room together. "I can't wait to see what Crystal has prepared for us."

They returned to the main part of the house—to the warm, clean air and the sounds of voices at work and play. And all around her, Vi felt something she had almost forgotten: the excited bustle of her family preparing for their trip to Viamede. Laughter spilled from the dining room where her sisters and brothers were already gathered.

As they approached the room, Vi squeezed her mother's hand and said, "Papa would be very happy for us tonight,

wouldn't he, Mamma? He was always so full of joy whenever we were about to leave on a journey."

"He would be happy for us," Elsie agreed. Then she added, "He would be happy for *you*, my darling."

# CHAPTER

**12**

# A New Face
# at Viamede

*But as for me and my
household, we will
serve the LORD.*

JOSHUA 24:15

# A New Face at Viamede

*S*everal days later, the travelers from Ion landed in the bustling port of New Orleans and were met by Mr. Mason, the chaplain at Viamede, and Mr. Mayhew, a lawyer who was Elsie's chief business representative in Louisiana. Elsie had decided not to stop in the Crescent City, where Mr. Mayhew lived, but to proceed immediately to Viamede. So their luggage was soon unloaded and transferred to another, smaller steamboat which would take the party back into the Gulf waters and up the Bayou Teche to Viamede. This final leg of the trip could be lengthy, but the weather was calm, and on the afternoon of the following day, the riverboat reached its destination.

From the plantation's dock, a wide gravel driveway led up a gentle, grassy slope to the house. The drive was lined with massive live oak trees whose branches trailed wispy fingers of moss and formed a canopied frame for the antebellum plantation house in the distance. The splendid white mansion with its broad balconies and verandas had not changed much in appearance since Elsie had lived there as a small child. In the afternoon sun, Viamede seemed to vibrate with light, beckoning the family forward.

An open carriage stood waiting at the dock for Molly, her mother, and Christine, who carried Danny. But the rest of the group chose to walk to the house. The twins and Rosemary ran ahead, bounding over the soft lawn and playing hide-and-seek around the old trees.

Watching them romp, Vi was reminded of her first visit to the plantation, when she was about five. She smiled at

her memories of chasing over this same lawn with her father; she could almost hear him laughing like a boy when he played tag with her, Missy, and Ed. And she realized for the first time that whenever it had been her turn to be "it," Papa would always let her catch him. It was a wonderful memory—one that just a few days ago would have been like a stab of pain to her troubled heart. For what must have been the hundredth time since the night in the luggage room with her mother, Vi said a silent prayer of thanks to the Lord for releasing her from the darkness of her guilt and doubt.

As they walked, Elsie and her parents chatted with Mr. Mason about the state of the plantation's many workers. When Elsie inquired about Aunt Mamie, the head housekeeper, Mr. Mason smacked his forehead in frustration and exclaimed, "How could I have forgotten? Mamie has been afflicted with circulation problems in her legs. Dr. Bayliss says that it is not too serious but could become worse if she does not rest. Between us, the doctor and I finally convinced her to give up her more taxing duties. We had to be quite firm, I can tell you. She wouldn't agree to curtail her activities until we found a temporary housekeeper of whom she approved. I say 'temporary' because we did not want to make a final decision without your approval, Mrs. Travilla."

"I do appreciate your concern," Elsie said, "but you say the person you hired meets Mamie's standards?"

"I was somewhat surprised at first," Mr. Mason continued. "We interviewed a number of highly qualified ladies, but Mamie found none to be wholly satisfactory. Then we interviewed Mrs. O'Flaherty, and Mamie took her on a tour of the house and kitchen as she did with all the applicants. When the

two returned to me, Mamie declared in no uncertain terms that Mrs. O'Flaherty was the one."

Rose asked the obvious question: "But why did Mamie's judgment surprise you, Mr. Mason?"

The chaplain's round face turned beet-red. "I am ashamed to say, ma'am, that I had not been impressed. But Mamie saw what I did not. If I had doubts, they were over-ridden first by Mamie and then by my good wife, who took to Mrs. O'Flaherty as quickly as Mamie did."

Mr. Mason came to a halt and shook his head in confusion. "Is it possible that women see one another differently than we men do? A most interesting idea. I must make a study of the subject," he said to himself. Then he picked up his pace and caught up to the others.

"How would you describe the new housekeeper, Mr. Mason?" inquired Horace, who had overheard the chaplain's short soliloquy and was struggling to suppress a chuckle.

"As a diamond in the rough, sir," said Mr. Mason. "I had appraised her more rough than diamond, but since she has taken up her duties here, I believe she is a gem. But you must judge for yourselves."

Their first view of Mrs. O'Flaherty came moments later as the woman emerged from the house and waved to the approaching crowd. *She does look a bit rough*, Elsie caught herself thinking.

Mrs. O'Flaherty hurried down the entrance steps, raising her calico skirts to ease her steps and in the process revealing a pair of highly polished, men's work boots and brightly patterned stockings. Elsie quickly raised her gaze up Mrs. O'Flaherty's tall frame (almost as tall as Horace) and broad shoulders to her head, which was as eccentric as

her feet. In the sunlight, her black hair, braided and coiled like a snake atop her head, seemed almost metallic blue. A brilliant smile showed an abundance of white teeth that sparkled in the light; on coming closer, Elsie realized that the sparkle came from one tooth in particular—a gold one in the center of the smile. Mrs. O'Flaherty's face was ruddy and furrowed about the eyes and mouth. But what really arrested Elsie's attention were the woman's eyes; they were large and clear and fringed with fine, black lashes, and the irises—made large in the daylight—were the pure blue of sapphires.

On reaching the large group, Mrs. O'Flaherty looked to Mr. Mason, and he responded with an introduction.

"Mrs. Travilla, I'd like you to meet Mrs. Maureen O'Flaherty, who has so kindly come to us as the temporary housekeeper of Viamede," he said with grave formality. "Mrs. O'Flaherty, this is Mrs. Travilla."

Elsie looked into the extraordinary face, and although she could not have explained her reaction, the mistress of Viamede instantly understood what Mamie and Mrs. Mason had seen there. Elsie extended her hand and received the grasp of a hand larger than her own and as firm as a man's. Even through her gloves, Elsie could feel the hardness of Mrs. O'Flaherty's palm—hardness that came from the calluses of labor.

But when Mrs. O'Flaherty spoke, Elsie experienced a new shock. The voice said only, "So glad to meet you, ma'am. Welcome home." But the sound of it was like music—rich, deep, and accented with Irish charm. Elsie, who had spent many years in the British Isles, recognized the accent instantly as that of a person raised in circumstances far more genteel than the life of a housemaid.

"Thank you, Mrs. O'Flaherty," Elsie replied courteously. Then she proceeded to make introductions to her father and mother and the rest. Each time Mrs. O'Flaherty replied to one or another of the party, they all felt a kind of thrill at the sound of her voice.

At last the housekeeper turned back to Elsie. "I've seen Miss Percival and her mother to the downstairs suite, ma'am. And your nursemaid to the little one's room. All the other rooms are ready, and the maids will unpack when your luggage is brought up. I can show you to your rooms now, but perhaps you would prefer the parlor. We have tea prepared—and cold lemonade for those who enjoy it."

At this last remark, she darted a look at the twins and Rosemary and winked.

"I think we would all like some refreshment," Elsie replied.

"We certainly shall," Horace agreed. He felt a tug on his jacket pocket and looked down. Rosemary stood beside him, and in the best whisper she could manage, she said, "I'm hungry, Grandpapa."

Mrs. O'Flaherty said, "I believe we can find a little something to satisfy you, Miss Rosemary. Perhaps you and your brothers would like to come with me."

Rosemary looked to her Mamma, who smiled and nodded. The child slipped her small hand into Mrs. O'Flaherty's large one. With a little curtsey to Elsie, Mrs. O'Flaherty departed, Rosemary at her side and Harold and Herbert close at her heels. As they entered the house, Elsie heard one of her sons ask the housekeeper, "Are you a pirate, Mrs. O'Flaherty?"

# Violet's Hidden Doubts

Mrs. O'Flaherty's "little something" turned out to be a luxurious spread for all the new arrivals. A variety of tasty sandwiches, cakes, and fresh fruits soon sated the appetites of all the travelers, and by the time they were shown to their rooms, their baggage had been delivered and the contents unpacked.

Vi was pleased to find that she would be sharing the suite of ground-floor rooms with Missy and her cousin Isa Conley. Molly and Aunt Enna occupied the other bedroom, which adjoined their common sitting room.

"Well, what do you think of Viamede?" Vi asked Isa, who was lounging on the couch in the sitting room.

"It's magnificent," Isa replied. "I never imagined a mansion this beautiful. Did you know that every bedroom in the house opens onto a porch or a balcony?"

"They're called 'galleries'," Missy explained, "and the doors open so the breezes can cool the whole house."

"And what do you both think of Mrs. O'Flaherty?" Vi asked mischievously. "Could she be a pirate, as Harold guessed?"

"One gold tooth does not a pirate make," Missy laughed. "She seems very kind and incredibly organized. She has a remarkably handsome face, too. I'm sure Lester would want to paint her."

"And her voice," Isa added. "I wouldn't be the least surprised to learn that she sings grand opera."

Vi dropped her eyes as she said, "I want to know more about her. How old is she? Where is she from? Her name and her accent speak of Ireland. I wonder if she has family there? Oh, is it very rude of me to be so curious?"

"Not at all," said Molly, who at that moment was wheeling her chair into the room. "Curiosity is a positive virtue in

126

my profession. What is rude is to let curiosity be satisfied with gossip and hasty conclusions. I, too, am very curious about Mrs. O'Flaherty, but I'm sure we will learn more about her as time goes on."

"Well, I'm curious about this gorgeous house," Isa said, flopping back against a pile of soft pillows. "It seems strange to have so beautiful a place without a family in residence."

"I think our Mamma is quite sentimental about Viamede," Missy commented. "It was the home of her mother, bought and renovated by her grandparents. Mamma and Papa spent their honeymoon here, and Papa loved the place as much as she. I often heard Papa lament the fact that so many of the great houses on the Teche have been abandoned or fallen into disrepair since the War. He wanted Viamede preserved, and he and Mamma felt they were in the best position to do that."

"Do Mr. and Mrs. Mason live in the house?" Molly wondered.

"They have their own house not far from here," Missy said.

"Oh, when may we have a tour of everything?" Isa asked eagerly.

"Tomorrow morning," Missy said. "We will see the whole house and the gardens. We can take a horseback ride, if you like. Mamma says there is a wonderful small cart, Molly, and she will have a driver ready if you want to accompany us."

"We could have a picnic in the orange grove. And then we can visit the little cemetery," Vi proposed. "It's not at all gloomy, but like a small park with monuments and benches and beautiful lawn and flowers. Mamma used to play there,

before she moved to Roselands. I played there too, when I was little."

The girls indeed got their full tour on the following day, from top to bottom of the grand old house and around the grounds. Molly and the twins joined them for their picnic. Their last stop, the tree-shaded cemetery where Elsie's mother and grandparents lay, proved to be just as Vi described. It was a lovely place to talk together and contemplate the splendor of a perfect April day—and what promised to be a perfect holiday for them all.

# CHAPTER

## 13

# New Friends and Complications

*Blessed is he who comes in
the name of the LORD!*

MARK 11:9

*T*hough the Travillas' state of mourning meant that there were no social events at Viamede, the young family members found plenty to occupy their time and were more than happy in one another's company. If boredom did threaten, they discovered that the remarkable Mrs. O'Flaherty always had a good idea for activities.

Elsie and her father spent their days primarily in discussions with the Viamede manager, Mr. Spriggs, and with Mr. Mason. She and Horace also made several business trips to New Orleans to meet with Mr. Mayhew and other lawyers and bankers there. But Elsie's primary concern was the hiring of a new manager and a new chaplain for Viamede. It seemed a daunting task: How could she hope to find employees of the uncommon character and loyalty of the two very different men who had served Viamede for so many years?

A new manager was the first priority. But the search for Mr. Spriggs's replacement proved surprisingly easy. A neighbor suggested they speak to a certain Mr. McFee. The name was immediately recognized, for had not a Mr. McFee and his wife taken over the running of Viamede during the War? The neighbor explained that this Mr. McFee was the nephew of the former manager. After several interviews, Elsie and Horace were fully satisfied with the young man's credentials and capabilities. He was offered the post and accepted immediately.

As for Mr. Mason and his good wife—was it possible that anyone could take their places? Were ever shepherds more attentive to their flock? Mr. Mason had seen to the

spiritual needs of the people of Viamede for more than twenty years now, and he still went about his duties with the gleeful enthusiasm he brought to the post when he was a fresh-faced theology student. Some years previously, Mr. Mason had taken on the additional responsibility of ministering to a local Protestant congregation, so that church was also losing its much-loved pastor.

Elsie wrote letters of inquiry to several schools of theology, and responses began to come in. She also conducted interviews with candidates recruited by Mr. Mayhew's associates, but none of these efforts produced candidates who seemed right to her.

The local congregation was conducting its own search, and from time to time, they engaged a visiting minister to conduct services. Just such a guest was in the pulpit on the first two Sundays that the family attended church. He seemed, to Elsie, a righteous man but too bound by the law to remember the compassion of grace and faith. Others of the congregation must have had similar feelings, for when the minister's visit was ended, he was not invited to stay on.

"We have another guest pastor coming on the second Sunday in May," Mr. Mason informed Elsie one day in late April. The expression on his face revealed such a confusion of hopefulness and anxiety that Elsie almost laughed. "I don't know his name," Mr. Mason said, "but he comes highly recommended."

Still, Elsie's experience thus far did not raise her hopes on that second Sabbath in May. She tried to keep an open mind, but as she settled into the family pew in the country church, her expectations were not high.

A neighbor—the same neighbor who had brought Mr. McFee to her attention—rose to introduce the visiting

minister. His name meant nothing to Elsie, but when it was said, Horace Dinsmore, who was seated beside her, gasped. She looked at her father and saw that an uncharacteristic flush had suffused his face. But before she could ask if he was well, Horace waved his hand to signal that he was fine.

The guest in the pulpit began to speak. His voice was strong, carrying to the farthest corner of the church, but melodious and full of warmth. His explication of the text for the day—Matthew 4:18-22, Jesus' calling of the first disciples to be "fishers of men"—was both intelligent and plainly stated, so that not even the youngest of the congregation were excluded from his message. So engaging was his sermon and so conversational his tone that Elsie hardly noticed his appearance until he finished speaking. But when the churchgoers rose for a final hymn and the benediction, given by Mr. Mason, she looked more closely and saw that the guest was younger than she had supposed—perhaps no more than twenty-seven or twenty-eight. He was handsome in a way that was not showy, with eyes the dark blue of the sea and hair a reddish-brown that caught the light through the church windows.

When the service ended, Elsie intended to hurry and catch the minister, for she hoped that he might join her family for luncheon that day. But a hand held her back.

"Let the others go first," Horace said in a low whisper.

So Elsie hung back with her father while Rose guided the rest of the family outside to meet the young pastor. Certainly there was a buzz in the church, and as people passed by her, Elsie listened.

"Most impressive"—"made me think"—"felt like he was talking straight to me"—"nearly as good as Mr. Mason, I'd say." The snatches of conversation that came to Elsie's ears

told her that her own response to the sermon was not unique. Even old Mrs. Caulkin was overheard to say, "A mite young but better than any other we've heard of late," which was high praise indeed from a woman who rarely had a good word for anyone or anything.

It was some time before the church was cleared out, but Horace finally nudged Elsie, and they made their way to the porch where the guest and Mr. Mason were standing.

Horace stepped forward and said, "Elsie dear, I would like you to meet the Reverend James Keith who is, if I am correct, a cousin of ours."

Elsie was dumbfounded. She looked first at her father, whose face wore an odd smile, then to the minister, who appeared no less surprised than herself. The younger man found his voice before she did and replied, "I believe I am, sir. I know that I am James Keith. If you are Horace Dinsmore, Jr., and this is Mrs. Travilla, then we are surely kin and there is no mistake."

Horace, forgetting protocol, took the young man's hand and began shaking it heartily. "You are Marcia's grandson and Cyril's son," he said. "Aunt Wealthy has written to me of the new preacher in the family."

"And she and my grandmother have told me of the Dinsmores," Mr. Keith responded. "I knew that you had property in this area, but I hardly expected—"

"Nor did we, Mr. Keith," Elsie said, for her father's mention of Aunt Wealthy Stanhope clarified something of this extraordinary meeting. "I'd planned to ask the visiting pastor to join us for lunch today. How much more exciting to invite a member of the family."

"Exciting indeed. Overwhelming," he said with obvious pleasure, but then his brow furrowed slightly. "But I must decline, Mrs. Travilla, for I am dining with my host, Mr. Embury, and his family."

"I would not be the barrier to a happy family reunion," came a deep voice from the foot of the porch stairs. Mr. Louis Embury, the neighbor who had brought Mr. McFee to Elsie's attention, climbed the steps. "Please, Mrs. Travilla," he said, "take my delightful houseguest with you. He will be staying with us for several weeks, and I believe we can share his company."

"Then you must join us too, Mr. Embury," Elsie said. "This reunion is apparently due to you, and I would not have you miss its outcome."

Mr. Embury, a widower in his early thirties, agreed. Elsie, suddenly remembering that Mr. Embury had young children, quickly included them in her invitation. But Mr. Embury declined on their behalf, for both his daughters were abed with spring colds.

"Perhaps Mr. and Mrs. Mason will ride with us," Mr. Embury said.

They all turned to the chaplain, whose normal river of words had literally ceased to flow (perhaps because his mind had been bubbling with ideas as he observed this chance encounter). He opened his mouth, but nothing came out. He gulped, tried again, and managed a "yes"—as high and shrill as a baby chick's peep.

He looked into the face of each person standing there, and a smile as joyful as a cherub's broke over his round face. "Thank You, dear Father and Savior," he proclaimed, "for what You have delivered to us this day! Thank You for family and friends and for this glorious morning and all the new opportunities it brings!"

Needless to say, luncheon at Viamede was not so quiet as on a normal Sabbath. The young people were only a little surprised to hear that the pastor and Mr. Embury would be at their table. But imagine their amazement on learning that the Reverend Keith was kindred — cousin to all the Travillas and their grandfather and great-grandfather.

"What should we call you?" Harold asked with some concern.

"I guess I should be 'Reverend Keith' or 'Mr. Keith' when we are at church," the newfound family member said with only slightly exaggerated seriousness. "But I prefer 'Cousin James' among family, if that suits you fellows."

"But what of us who are not related?" Molly asked.

"If it is not too forward, I would like to be cousin to all, for blood is not the only measure of family."

So Cousin James was welcomed to Viamede and into the hearts of everyone there. He became a frequent visitor — often accompanied by Mr. Embury. Both men were sincerely respectful of the family's mourning, yet James sensed that their visits were no burden at Viamede. And the contacts with so many sociable and interesting ladies and gentlemen were good for Louis Embury, who had lost his wife only two years previously.

Besides, James was an instant favorite with Mr. and Mrs. Mason, who showed him every aspect of Viamede, with special emphasis on its spiritual life. By the time he delivered his next sermon in the local church, James was well aware that Mr. Mason's interest was not without its hidden motives. The church needed a new pastor; the plantation needed a new chaplain; and Mr. Mason clearly

needed to know that he would be leaving his Viamede congregation and the church in good hands.

When James realized that he was in the running for both
positions, he began thinking seriously about the prospect of
making his home in Louisiana. A Midwesterner by birth,
educated in the East, he had never contemplated a ministry
in the South. He'd come to the region only as a tourist,
accepting an invitation from Louis Embury, whom he had
met through one of his seminary instructors.

On the afternoon following his second Sunday sermon,
James was sitting with Molly, Missy, Vi, and Isa on the
veranda of Viamede. The young women were telling him
about the informal Bible study group they had started and
received his promise to attend their next gathering.

"Might we meet tomorrow?" Vi asked.

Molly and Isa quickly agreed, but Missy interrupted them,
saying, "I have nearly forgotten. Oh, where is my head?"

"In Italy, I suspect," Isa laughed. "But what have you
forgotten?"

"Mamma plans to go to New Orleans tomorrow and stay
for a few days. She will visit Mr. and Mrs. Carpenter at
their mission, and she wants to know if we would like to
accompany her. We will return on Friday."

"Where will we stay?" Vi asked.

"With Mr. and Mrs. Mayhew," Missy said. "Mrs. Mayhew
has volunteered to give us a tour of the city."

"Is there some other reason for this visit?" Vi inquired,
for she thought her mother's business in New Orleans had
been completed.

"I don't know," Missy replied. "Yesterday, Mamma
received letters from Dinah and Mrs. Mayhew. And that's
when she decided to make the trip."

Vi said only, "Oh," but she sensed that there was something more in this hurried journey.

"Is this Mrs. Carpenter an old friend of yours?" James inquired.

"Yes, and more," Vi said. "She is the granddaughter of our Aunt Chloe."

"Another family member?" James asked.

A faint blush touched Missy's face. "Chloe was a slave, and she cared for our mother from the moment she was born," Missy explained in a soft tone. "She cared for me and Vi and the rest when we were small. She is not kin, though I wish she were, for we love her—and her husband—with all our hearts."

"But surely the affection you have is good?" James said, for he had observed the downcast eyes of the other girls as Missy spoke.

"Oh, I guess we are all embarrassed to admit that our Aunt Chloe was ever a slave," Vi responded. "You see, Cousin James, our parents never believed in slavery, and they did their best to fight it. They broke the law by educating their workers, and Papa even supported the fugitive slave movement before the War. But they couldn't put an end to the system by themselves, so they owned slaves until the War abolished the system."

"Please do not think me impertinent," James said hesitantly, "but may I ask why slaveowners who believed slavery wrong did not free their slaves? Would that not have set the example for others to follow?"

"It would not have been as easy as it sounds," Vi said. "Even in the North, freed slaves were subject to capture and being brought back to the South and sold into bondage again. Before the War, white people who espoused abolition here

were also in grave danger. Even after the War, our papa was the special target of violent men who wanted the old system restored. They tried to kill Papa and burn our house."

"I didn't know," James said. "I regret reviving memories that are so painful."

"You have nothing to regret," Isa said. There was a quaver in her voice that betrayed her strong emotion. "I, for one, do not want to forget those times. We must never forget the pain or the injustice of treating our fellow human beings as slaves. Never! For what we forget, we are more likely to repeat."

James stared at Isa, seeing for the first time beneath her lovely appearance. *There is steel in this girl*, he thought.

"We're glad to discuss this subject with you, Cousin James," Missy said. "Some people think it's not proper for ladies and girls to talk of politics and the problems that plague our society, but we are more advanced than that."

Molly then added, "I wish you could have known Missy and Vi's father, for Cousin Edward was an extraordinary man. He believed without reservation in the equality of all, and he taught each of us to respect our minds and use them."

James said, "I would like to continue the discussion. There is a great deal I must learn about the South and its unhappy history. My attitudes have been shaped from afar, yet I begin to understand that my thinking has been too simple."

Elsie, who had come onto the veranda in time to hear the last part of this conversation, walked forward. Catching sight of her, James rose and offered his seat.

"Thank you, Cousin James," she said, taking her place in the group. "Missy, have you told everyone about our plans for tomorrow?"

"Yes, Mamma," Missy replied.

"Well, I'm hoping our Cousin James might join us if his schedule permits," Elsie said, smiling graciously at James. "I think you would be interested in the work that Reverend and Mrs. Carpenter are doing. Like you, they have chosen to devote their lives to the ministry."

"Oh, please come with us," Vi begged excitedly.

The others joined her in encouraging their cousin to accept, though in truth James required little persuading. "I should like very much to join you," he said. "But will it be an imposition on your friends, the Mayhews? I can easily stay at a hotel."

Elsie assured him, "I am sure they can find a room for another of the Dinsmore clan."

"Or a large wardrobe if there is no room," Vi giggled.

As it turned out, one of the group was missing the next morning when they boarded the riverboat for the voyage to New Orleans. Molly had decided not to make the trip, for the weather had turned very warm and she feared becoming fatigued by travel. So she chose to stay at Viamede with her mother and Horace and Rose.

"Do you think Molly is feeling sick?" Vi asked as she and Isa stood on the deck of the boat, watching the Viamede dock disappear around the turn in the river.

"Not in the way you mean," Isa replied with a knowing smile. "I'm not worried about her health."

At Vi's quizzical look, Isa said, "Did you know that Aunt Rose has invited Mr. Embury and his daughters to dine at Viamede today?"

"But what has that to do with Molly?" Vi asked.

"Perhaps nothing," Isa said. "Perhaps everything. Oh, I'm sorry. I do not mean to sound like an old gossip, but I have noticed that Mr. Embury seems to take a special interest in our Molly's company."

"Um," was Vi's only response, for this was an observation she had missed.

The lush bayou landscape flowed past, its panoply of cypress, palmetto, thick vines, and water flowers interrupted occasionally by stretches of pasture and low-lying rice paddies. Isa said, "I had not realized there were so many shades of green in nature."

"I think you may be right," Vi said, still pondering Isa's observation about Mr. Embury and Molly.

"God has truly painted this country with a magnificent palette," Isa commented.

"He has," Vi said, "but I was talking about Mr. Embury. I think you may be right. Now that you mention it, he is very attentive to Molly when he visits. I often see them deep in conversation, and Molly told me that she has read some of her poems to him. You know how reserved she is about her poetry. She won't even hear suggestions that she publish it."

Isa laughed, "So I am not the only gossip."

"This isn't gossip," Vi protested. "We are merely comparing notes. Don't we have a responsibility to guard our cousin's happiness?"

"We do," Isa agreed, "but we must not rush into judgments based on speculation. That's my mother's specialty, and I know what harm it can do. I want to think that Molly can find love. I want to think we all can—as Missy has—find loving helpmates to share our days. But I believe Molly

has convinced herself that marriage is denied to her because of her handicap."

"Maybe she needs to make a study of these greens," Vi said.

Now it was Isa's turn to be confused. At her questioning look, Vi said, "I've learned about color from trying to paint it. Look around, and you'll see green everywhere, because that's what you expect to see. But scrunch up your eyes like this"—she demonstrated by contorting her face—"and you can see yellows and blues, purples and reds, browns and black. The green is really made up of lots of colors and of light and shadow. That's what people are like. God makes us in endless variations. If we look only for green—for a single quality in others—then we miss the real beauty of each variation God has made."

"That's a lovely metaphor," Isa said. She squinted her eyes and stared into the thick vegetation along the river's bank. In this way, she saw what Vi was talking about—a kaleidoscope of colors wheeling and dancing before her. She held her gaze until her eyes began to hurt and she blinked.

"It's like magic, isn't it?" Vi said. "But it isn't magic because God has made all this color for us to see, if we will only use our eyes. 'Man looks at the outward appearance, but the Lord looks at the heart,'" she said, quoting a familiar verse of Scripture.

Turning back to her younger cousin, Isa said, "Perhaps Mr. Embury is the type of man who looks beneath the surface to see all the colors hidden in the green. But whatever his feelings, I pray that our Molly can look beyond her crippled legs and see the wealth of beauty and intelligence and love she has to give."

That afternoon, as the riverboat plowed its way toward the Gulf, a most pleasant outing was underway back at Viamede. Under the watchful eyes of Horace and Rose, four children—Rosemary, Danny, and the two energetic Embury girls, whose names were Corinne and Madeline ("Maddie" for short)—played in the shade of the orange grove. Not too far away, the girls' father carefully pushed a wheeled chair and its occupant along a hard dirt path to a small glade formed by a semicircle of crepe myrtle trees.

Stopping to rest, Mr. Embury sat on the grass, and he and Molly talked of many things, for he was a man of excellent education and shared many of Molly's interests in literature and art and music. By chance, the subject of his marriage was raised when he mentioned his late wife's passion for opera.

Molly asked, in total innocence, "Would you ever consider marrying again, Mr. Embury, for your children?"

He paused, and Molly was suddenly and painfully aware of the impertinence of so personal a question. But Mr. Embury took no offense.

"Until recently, I would have said no," he replied slowly. "And I should still say the same if you mean would I marry only to give my youngsters the benefit of a mother. I believe that true love between husband and wife is among the greatest gifts that God gives us. The love of two parents for one another serves as the model of marriage when their children grow up and choose their own life partners."

Molly, her cheeks burning in a reaction that had nothing to do with the temperature, stammered, "I—I'm so sorry, Mr. Embury. I had no right to ask..."

"You have every right, Miss Percival, as my friend. I do count you as a friend, and I value your forthrightness."

"Still…"

"My answer to your question is yes, I would marry again."

"What has changed your mind, Mr. Embury?"

He looked off to some distant point and said, "Time, perhaps. They say it is the great healer. Time and…" He hesitated.

Turning back to look into Molly's eyes, he smiled. "But let's just leave it at that, Miss Percival. For now."

# CHAPTER 14

# Seeing New Orleans

*Through the blessing of the upright a city is exalted....*

PROVERBS 11:11

Vi tugged her thin bathrobe close and rapped lightly on the door of Elsie's sleeping cabin.

At the sound of her mother's questioning "Yes?" Vi entered.

Vi approached the small berth and sat down. Seeing the open Bible on Elsie's lap, she said, "Did I interrupt your prayers, Mamma?"

"No, dear. I was just searching for some inspiration. But tell me what brings you to my side at so late an hour. Couldn't you sleep?"

"No, ma'am," Vi replied in a voice so sweet it sounded like a child's. "I've been thinking about you. You've been working so hard since we got to Viamede. And tonight, for the first time, I saw that you looked tired, and I'm worried about you."

Elsie extended her arm and drew Vi close. "I admit it," she said. "This visit has been tiring. But I promise you, darling, that I am just fine. A person can be tired without being ill, so there's no cause for you to worry."

Vi snuggled close. "I don't want you to be sick, Mamma. I just can't bear the thought of your being sick or—or…"

"Or of my dying?"

Soft tears began to trickle from Vi's eyes as she said, "Or that. To think of a world without Papa and you. It's horrible. Just too horrible."

"Oh, my darling, you must trust that I would not jeopardize my health any more than yours," Elsie said. "I'd sell Viamede tomorrow if doing its business were too much for me."

She put her hand under Vi's chin and lifted her daughter's face. With a smile, she went on, "I'm a very sensible woman, you know. And besides, I'm not planning to leave you for a long time unless the Lord has need of me. I'm always prepared to answer His call, but being ready is not the same as being silly enough to ignore common sense."

Vi brushed away her tears. "Sometimes I think that I think too much," she sniffled.

This drew a warm laugh from her mother. "Not too much by any means," she said. "I want you to be thoughtful, but it is wise not to anticipate the worst before you have contemplated other possibilities. I am tired because I've been working hard, but I also feel satisfied with what has been accomplished. Viamede's business is in excellent shape, just as your father left it. We have employed Mr. McFee, and I have a feeling we may soon have a new chaplain."

Vi had already guessed her mother's choice. "Then you've asked Cousin James to stay at Viamede?" she asked.

Elsie's eyes opened wide in amused surprise. "No, I haven't spoken to Cousin James yet, and don't you breathe a word of this to him. I still must consult with the congregation at Viamede. If that goes well, I will offer the post to James. But I do not want him to feel pressured. He never planned to come to the South to live, and this will be a difficult decision for him, I'm sure. He must feel free to choose what is best for him. So let's keep this matter strictly between the two of us for now."

"Of course, Mamma," Vi pledged, feeling quite mature enough to share an important confidence with her mother.

"Are you ready for sleep?" Elsie asked. "If we both look tired at breakfast, the others are sure to notice, and one worrier is all I really need."

"May I ask one more question?"

"A quick one."

"This trip was so sudden. Is something wrong with Dinah?"

Elsie settled back against her pillow, still holding her daughter close. "Dinah and her family are all well," she said. "But I do have plans beyond seeing the sights of New Orleans. I want us to spend some time at the mission, so I asked Dinah if we could visit for a day or two. I think it's important for you girls to see the work that the Carpenters are doing."

"And Cousin James, too?" Vi asked.

Elsie smiled and said, "Yes, Cousin James, too. He should meet the Carpenters, for they can provide a perspective on the South that is very different from mine. But this visit is for the benefit of us all, dear. I've been giving a lot of thought to the mission and what we can do to help Dinah and Mr. Carpenter with their work."

"You gave money, didn't you?" Vi asked.

"Yes, dear. Your Papa and I gave funds to start the mission and acquire the property where it is located, but there are needs that money alone cannot meet," Elsie said. "The point is to do what will genuinely benefit the Carpenters and all the people who are served at the mission. Your Papa always said that the best way to know another person is to walk in his shoes for awhile, and that's what I hope we will all try to do."

Vi thought for a few moments, then she said, "I understand, Mamma. To serve others, a person has to do more than just talk about it. We have to *live* God's commandment—truly live it every day. Jesus told us to love our neighbors as ourselves, and loving others means understanding

and respecting them, doesn't it? Because that's how we want to be treated."

"I believe it does," Elsie said. "To love others, we have to care about them. And when we really care about someone, we try to understand that person's heart. That's what your Papa meant about walking in another person's shoes. We can't *be* another person, but we can try to look beyond appearances and better understand what is inside."

Elsie hugged her daughter close and added, "I am very glad you decided to visit with me tonight. Your father and I so often talked like this after you and your sisters and brothers were tucked in bed at night. You have reminded me of how helpful it is to open my heart to a kindred spirit."

"Thank you, Mamma, for asking me on this trip," Vi said as she kissed Elsie's cheek and stood to go back to her own cabin. "It's a very grown-up kind of trip, isn't it?"

"I knew you were ready for it," Elsie said. "But go to your bed now. We both need our sleep, for we have several very busy days ahead."

When Vi was snugly back in her own berth, she had a thought just before she fell asleep: *Maybe growing up won't be so bad after all, if I can be like Mamma and always find ways to help others.*

The boat trip was delayed by many stops to pick up cargo along the way. So Elsie and her young companions arrived in the port city later than expected the next afternoon. They were met by Mr. Mayhew and driven directly to his home in one of the most beautiful residential sections of the city.

Mrs. Mayhew—a small, stout woman with a personality as outgoing as her husband's was staid—greeted them with hugs, a delicious meal, and plans for the next day. Elsie would accompany Mr. Mayhew to a final meeting with her business managers, and the others would be entirely in Mrs. Mayhew's hands. During supper, Mrs. Mayhew previewed her sightseeing itinerary, and all her young houseguests were excited by this opportunity to see the city, even Vi and Missy. Though they'd both visited New Orleans on a number of occasions, they'd never had a full-fledged tour with so jovial a guide as Mrs. Mayhew.

"I will run you young people ragged tomorrow," Mrs. Mayhew promised as she bid them good night. "Now, be sure to wear your coolest frocks, girls, and don't forget your parasols. The carriage will be open so you can have the best views, but our New Orleans sun will bake you like muffins if you don't have your parasols."

The tour began bright and early, and the visitors quickly discovered that their hostess was as well informed as she was affable. Mrs. Mayhew was a native Orleanian, and she regaled them with the kind of stories that made the city's history come alive. She told them about the first French settlers and how French rule had given way to Spanish. As they reached the French Quarter, the streets narrowed, and Mrs. Mayhew explained that this was the oldest residential part of the city. The houses seemed small compared to those in the Mayhews' neighborhood; "but don't be deceived," the good lady warned. "These houses extend far back, with magnificent gardens in the rear. When the French developed this crescent of land formed by the Mississippi River, they adopted the style of their homeland, building on long, narrow lots and erecting gated walls in front. Where the

gates are open, look through and you will see the open courtyards."

"Some of the houses look almost Spanish," Missy observed.

"You have a good eye," Mrs. Mayhew said. "Have you heard the term 'Creole'? It's a French word that refers to the people of European origin who settled in the New World and to their descendants. Here in New Orleans, Creole means a person of both French and Spanish descent. It also applies to architecture and foods—oh, so many things where the two cultures have mixed and blended over a century and a half."

"Are you a Creole, Mrs. Mayhew?" Vi asked.

"No, I'm an American," the lady replied. "You may think it odd I say that, because we are all Americans. But when Napolean Bonaparte secretly sold the Louisiana Territory to the United States in 1803, the Creole citizens were none too happy to learn about it. Many of them regarded the Americans who flooded into the city as barbarians and would not associate with the newcomers except by necessity. And that sense of division is still with us, though it is softening with each new generation. I have many Creole friends, but there are a few old-timers who still long to see the French flag flying over our city hall in place of the Stars and Stripes."

She then told them about the other waves of immigrants—German, Irish, Caribbean, Chinese, Italian—who had made New Orleans the most international city in all the United States, by her reckoning. "When Mr. Mayhew and I first traveled to Paris many years ago," she chuckled, "I wondered why we had bothered, for it seemed just like home. I was quite young," she added as explanation, "but

I soon realized that New Orleans is not Paris nor Madrid nor any other place, but a unique blend of all the influences that its people brought from their native lands."

Their first stop was Jackson Square, where the statue of Andrew Jackson overlooked the tourists as they walked about. Posed on the back of a rearing horse, the hero of the Battle of New Orleans in the War of 1812 seemed to be raising his hat in salute to the three towers of the St. Louis Cathedral. Mrs. Mayhew told them that the congregation had been active since the early 1700s, though the church had been destroyed twice—first by a hurricane, then by fire—and that the current structure had been extensively remodeled before the Civil War.

They proceeded next to the Ursuline convent not far away, and Mrs. Mayhew told how the nuns of the Ursuline Order had arrived in the 1720s after the most harrowing ocean voyage, bringing medical care and education to the settlement. "I doubt there would be a New Orleans without the Sisters of Ursula," Mrs. Mayhew said. "There is no counting the number of lives those good women have saved. And no words can convey their bravery in the face of every kind of disaster."

The carriage was halted before the convent building, which was one of the oldest in the United States, and Mrs. Mayhew's expression became serious. Her voice deepened as she said, "Our city is often characterized as a place devoted to worldly pleasures. But it was founded on faith, and the love of the Lord is strong here. You will see churches of every religion today, and the people who worship in them are strong in faith. It's not easy to live in a city that was built on a swamp and protected from the waters of the Mississippi only by earthen levees. The people of New

Orleans have endured unimaginable suffering—hurricanes from the Gulf that have swept away everything in their paths, fires that have consumed entire areas of the city, and worst of all, the epidemics of yellow fever, typhoid, and other raging plagues that can take hundreds of thousands of lives in just a few weeks. But with each trial, our Heavenly Father has strengthened the people and supported them as they rebuilt and recovered. Today, New Orleans is a prosperous city, yet the dangers of epidemics and natural disaster are always with us. It is not worldly pleasure that enables the people to endure. It is faith, my dears, the shield and helmet of faith."

They were all silent for some moments. Looking again at the low buildings that had housed the religious women who served God by caring for the sick and the poor and the abandoned, Vi thought of her conversation with her mother on the riverboat. With no regard for their own safety or comfort, those women had *lived* their faith through service to others.

As she marveled at the steadfast courage of the Sisters of Ursula, Vi heard Mrs. Mayhew giving instructions to the carriage driver. She turned to her companions and saw that a cheery smile again reigned on Mrs. Mayhew's face. "Our next stop is the old St. Louis cemetery on Basin Street," the lady was saying. "You must see how Orleanians honor their dead. Then we will have our lunch at my favorite Creole restaurant."

The cemetery with its above-ground tombs and mausoleums was fascinating. And lunch was leisurely and as delicious as Mrs. Mayhew said it would be. But she would not let them rest for long. Their next stop was an imposing building on Bourbon Street—the French Opera House.

Mrs. Mayhew spoke about the love of music that, she said, "was woven in the city's fabric." A man at the door agreed to let them inside for a peek, and as they stood in the huge auditorium, Mrs. Mayhew described how the rows of seats could be removed for grand balls. "You should see it during Mardi Gras," she said, "when this room is filled with music and dancing and people in the most elaborate costumes. In my younger days, I quite enjoyed the fancy dress balls, and you can't imagine how handsome Mr. Mayhew was in his evening attire," she chuckled.

At last they headed back toward the Mayhews' residence. On the wide thoroughfare of Saint Charles Street, they saw all the evidence of prosperity—splendid hotels, office buildings, and theaters. Then along the residential streets, they passed many beautiful homes, some almost as grand as Viamede, and lush gardens that were truly breathtaking. Mrs. Mayhew seemed to know the history of every house and all the families who had ever dwelled there.

Reaching the Mayhews', they found Elsie waiting in the back garden, ready with cooling drinks and a listening ear. Before excusing themselves to dress for dinner, the young people excitedly told her about all they had seen and learned on their excursion.

When Elsie and Mrs. Mayhew were alone, Elsie expressed her gratitude to her old friend.

"Oh, we only scratched the surface," Mrs. Mayhew said. "The French Quarter, Saint Charles Street, and the old St. Louis cemetery. They were amazed by the tombs, as all our visitors are. I talked their poor ears off, of course," she laughed.

"Their ears all seemed intact," Elsie said, joining in the laughter. "And they clearly learned a great deal from you. I

heard Vi referring to the sidewalks as *banquettes*, just like a born Orleanian."

Mrs. Mayhew's expression changed as she said, "I think tomorrow will be even more eventful. At the mission, they will see another side of the city. It will be a powerful contrast. If my impression of your daughters and their friends is correct, our little tour today will soon pale in comparison to the wealth of love and self-sacrifice they will experience at the mission. I have never properly thanked you, dear Elsie, for introducing me to the Carpenters. They have opened my eyes again to what is possible when people walk in the footsteps of the Lord and live their faith."

# CHAPTER

15

# Days at the Mission

*For you know the grace of our LORD Jesus Christ, that though he was rich, yet for your sakes he became poor....*

2 CORINTHIANS 8:9

# Days at the Mission

*T*he next two days of the New Orleans visit were spent at the mission. The mission's neighborhood was a far cry from the Mayhews'. There were no beautiful houses and lush gardens. Most of the dwellings were old and in bad repair, their tin roofs rusting away in the humid climate. The streets were unpaved and would turn into rivers of mud when it rained. The mission itself was in an old warehouse, a brick structure that seemed as solid as the houses around it were flimsy. The building had been recently painted, and its door was a warm red that provided the only color amid the sun-bleached surroundings.

Dinah was waiting at the door when the carriage pulled up. She called for her husband and ushered the visitors inside. It was a happy reunion, for Vi and Missy hadn't seen the Carpenters in a number of years. Elsie introduced Isa and James. Then Mr. Carpenter called for attention and took a sheet of paper from his pocket.

"Your mother has told us that you young people want to see for yourselves how our mission is run," Mr. Carpenter began. "Well, seeing is one thing and doing is another. I can just tell that you are all doers, so I made this list of chores that need doing. You can put your bonnets and purses in my office and decide among yourselves what jobs you'd like to begin with. And Mr. Keith, I have a task for you as well."

Then Dinah addressed Elsie: "I was hoping you might join me in the classroom this morning. My students are starting to arrive even now, and we provide breakfast for them. I learned a long time ago that children can't learn when their stomachs are empty."

# Violet's Hidden Doubts

Elsie was very happy with her assignment, and she followed Dinah to the mission kitchen where trays of fresh-baked rolls, fruit, and milk had been prepared for Dinah's pupils. Missy wanted to help with the day's cooking, and she accompanied her mother and Dinah. Mr. Carpenter introduced Isa to Mary Johnson, a young woman whom she would assist to sort large piles of donated clothing and blankets. Vi chose to help with the little children, so Mr. Carpenter put her under the capable supervision of an older woman named Mrs. Duke. With the young ladies settled into their duties, Mr. Carpenter said to James, "You best roll up your sleeves, Mr. Keith. You and I are going out back. There's a pile of wood that needs chopping to keep that old kitchen stove hot. We serve a lot of empty stomachs here day and evening."

Mrs. Duke was a grandmotherly woman who told Vi that this was "doctor day" at the mission. A physician from one of the hospitals came in for the morning and conducted a clinic for the poor. "It's mostly mothers and children," Mrs. Duke explained. "While the mammas are seeing the doctor, we look after the little ones. I hope you like to read, Miss Violet, 'cause that's what the little ones just love. Most of them never see a book except when they come here."

She showed Vi the small collection of picture books that she kept in a closet, and Vi selected several. Then they went to the entry hall of the building. Four women were waiting for the doctor. Each had a baby on her lap, and half a dozen children played at their feet. Mrs. Duke talked with the women, writing their names on a small pad and asking about any special problems. Vi wasn't sure what to do, so she sat down on the bottom step of the hall stairs. She opened a book of fairy tales and pretended to read to her-

self. The children seemed to be paying no attention to her, though from the corner of her eye, Vi saw them casting shy glances in her direction. Not two minutes passed before a small hand touched her knee.

"Whatcha doin', lady?" a girl of about four asked.

"Reading a story," Vi said, smiling at the child.

"'Bout what?"

"It's about a boy and some magic beans," Vi replied. "Would you like to hear it?"

The little girl said nothing, but she sat down beside Vi on the stairway and looked at the book. Vi pointed to the drawing on the page. "See, that's the boy. His name is Jack, and that's his cow. He's supposed to sell his cow for money to buy food for himself and his poor mother. But he decides to trade the cow for some beans."

Another child had come close, a dark-eyed boy of five or so, and he said, "That's dumb. A whole cow for some beans?"

The boy slipped past the little girl and sat on the step above Vi, so he could look over her shoulder at the picture. "You gonna read that book?" he asked.

"I can read it to you, if you like," Vi said.

The girl said, "Yes, please ma'am," and scooted close to Vi. The boy said, "I guess that's okay," in a nonchalant tone, but he too moved closer.

Vi began to read and soon all the children were gathered around her, rapt in the tale of Jack and the Beanstalk. When she finished, the boy at her shoulder said, "That's a pretty good story, I think. Do you know any more?"

"Oh, I know lots of stories," Vi said. "I can read another, or I can tell you one."

"Tell one, miss," begged a curly-haired girl at her feet.

Vi thought for a moment, then asked, "Do you all know about Jesus?"

The small heads bobbed enthusiastically, and Vi went on, "Well, when Jesus was a boy of twelve, he went with his parents to Jerusalem...."

For the next three hours, Vi read and told stories, welcoming each new child who arrived and bidding a fond farewell to them when they left with their mothers. She also talked with the little ones, just as her mother did with Danny and Rosemary, and she was delighted at how bright and curious they all were.

She remarked on this to Mrs. Duke, and the kindly lady said, "The shame is they have so few opportunities to learn. Some of them may get to go to Mrs. Carpenter's school, but nobody else cares about educating those sweet angels. The children you met today are lucky, Miss Violet. They've got mothers who do everything they can for their babies. But there's plenty who have no parents and no one to care. You see them in the streets, begging, and you see them as young as seven and eight working at jobs no self-respecting adult would take on. Sometimes they show up here, asking for a meal or a bit of clothing—boys and girls who've had all the brightness and curiosity sapped away by poverty. It's such a waste of good lives, a real tragedy. But this mission, well, it's bringing some hope into lots of lives."

Vi had many questions she wanted to ask, but Mrs. Duke had other chores to do before she left for the day. Later, Vi learned from Mr. Carpenter that Mrs. Duke was a volunteer. She helped at the mission every morning while her own grandchildren had their lessons with Dinah. Mrs. Duke and her husband, a dock worker, were raising their

five grandchildren and also caring for Mr. Duke's elderly mother.

"They're good people," Mr. Carpenter said. "They don't ask anything for themselves except the chance to do what they can for others."

～

After her morning classes, Dinah paid visits to some of the older and infirm people in the neighborhood—taking food and medicines to those who could not get out on their own. James offered to accompany Dinah on her rounds, and so did Vi and Isa. As they were setting off, Vi overheard a teenaged boy gruffly expressing his opinion of inexperienced "society folk who come down here to parade their fancy clothes."

That remark and several others she heard troubled her, and on the second morning at the mission, Vi deliberately sought out the Reverend Carpenter. She found him in his tiny office behind the mission's kitchen.

"May I speak to you, Mr. Carpenter?" she asked. "I don't want to interrupt, so I can come back later."

"You're not interrupting, Miss Travilla," he replied, his deep voice as welcoming as his wide smile. "I was making some notes for my Sunday sermon, and I just finished."

He motioned her to a chair near his desk and asked, "Now, how can I help you?"

Vi took a breath and said, "I've been thinking about your mission and our being here. It means so much to us to take part in the work you're doing, but are we really helping? I mean, I heard some people yesterday say something about 'society women' and 'rich folks' and, well, it made me worry and I wanted to ask you…"

Vi didn't complete her sentence, for in truth she wasn't quite sure what she wanted to ask.

The minister's expression grew serious. "I think I understand," he said gently. "You're afraid that people here might misread your motives and resent you because you're wealthy and they're poor."

"That's it, Mr. Carpenter," Vi said. "That's exactly it."

Mr. Carpenter leaned back in his chair and said, "It's a big question, and one I often ponder on myself. Rich and poor alike, we're all one in the eyes of the Lord, but not necessarily in each other's eyes. I imagine that yesterday and today, maybe you've been feeling the difference that money can make. And wondering why you have so much when the people you meet here have so little."

Vi's eyes widened as she said, "Last night I read again the story of the rich young man in Matthew. Jesus told him to sell his possessions and give to the poor. I'm rich by the world's standards, but I have no possessions of my own to sell. What can I do to make life better for others? How can I really help people who haven't been as blessed as I?"

Mr. Carpenter stroked his chin for several seconds. Then he said, "Miss Travilla, it's as plain as day that you want to do good, but you aren't sure how. These past two days, you've seen and heard things you've never experienced before — met people so poor they may go hungry for days or have to beg from strangers to feed their children. These are things you've known about in your head, but now they are real for you in your heart. And you want to change those things, don't you?"

Vi looked up and said, "Yes, sir, I do. I want the children to have plenty to eat and warm clothes to wear. I want them to go to school. I want their mothers not to have to work so

hard night and day. And I want the old people we visited yesterday to have doctors and medicine when they're sick, just as I do. But it's so unfair!"

Mr. Carpenter agreed. "Unfair, yes. But unfair because people make it that way—not God. That's one of God's challenges for us. Each of us, rich and poor, has to follow His commandment to love our neighbors as ourselves. You and your family have been blessed with material wealth. That's a fact. And there's a reason for it—God's reason. He wants you to do something with what you have, and you've got to figure out what."

Vi nodded and sighed.

"You have good examples all around you," Mr. Carpenter continued. "None better than your own mother. She and your father donated all the funds to start this mission, and they brought others into the project. Did you know that Mrs. Mayhew is one of our biggest supporters?"

Vi's expression showed her surprise, and Mr. Carpenter explained, "Mrs. Mayhew is a hard worker, though the people we help here wouldn't know it. She has a talent for convincing wealthy folks to do what's right. First thing she did for us was to convince the hospital to provide doctors for our clinic. Then she and Mr. Mayhew got some church leaders together, and the next thing you know, we've got Bibles for our services and a good piano, too. Right now, she's raising money so we can employ a nurse full time. When you get right down to it, Mrs. Mayhew and her husband aren't much different from Mrs. Duke and her husband. The Mayhews have more material wealth than the Dukes could dream of, but they've all got God in their hearts."

Mr. Carpenter went on, "I can't tell you exactly how you can best help others. Our Heavenly Father sets out different

paths for each of us. But you talk with Him from your heart, and He'll show you the way. Now, don't be expecting the answers to come overnight. You've got to experience life to know how to live it. You've got to listen carefully and look inside other people, get to know them deep down, and let them help you understand what they really need."

"But what if I can't help?" Vi said.

"When you came to my door, you were worried about people taking your presence here the wrong way. The truth is, some people will do just that. They might resent you and turn away your help. And along the way, you'll meet some folks who just won't let you get close enough to help. But keep your heart open and don't get discouraged. There are as many ways to do for others as there are people who need help. Giving money is just one way, and not always the best one. You talk to the Lord and let Him guide you. He'll give you more ideas than you ever dreamed of—at least He has always done that for me."

Mr. Carpenter paused and smiled to himself. Then he said, "This mission was His idea. I'd never have thought of staying in the South, but God led me to Dinah. She told me about New Orleans and the need for people of goodwill and faith down here. Together, we talked to God, and He planted the seed of this service in our hearts."

"And do you ever get discouraged?" Vi asked.

He laughed, "About a dozen times every day. But God is always with me, telling me to go on." He rose from his chair, saying, "I get down, and He lifts me up. He never fails me."

Vi stood up quickly. "Oh, I've taken too much of your time," she apologized anxiously.

"Not at all," he said. "You're a thoughtful young lady, Miss Travilla, and I'm complimented that you wanted to

share your thoughts with me. I don't have absolute answers for you, but I can tell by your questions that you are setting out on the right track."

At that moment, Mrs. Duke looked in the open door. "There you are," she said cheerfully to Vi. "Several of the children you read to yesterday have come back, and they're begging me to find you. They want more stories."

"See that, Miss Travilla?" Mr. Carpenter said. "Opportunities to help are always looking for us."

Vi made a quick curtsey and said, "Thank you, Mr. Carpenter. Thank you so very much!" And she hurried away to her new young friends.

---

Early in the afternoon, Elsie was able to take both the Carpenters aside to thank them for the visit.

"These two days have meant a great deal to all of us," she said. "But they have been especially meaningful for Vi. Her father's death has been so hard for her, much harder than I realized until recently. Chloe told me that a visit here would help to get Vi out of the doldrums and back to her old self again."

"If I may say so, Mrs. Travilla," Mr. Carpenter said, "I don't believe your daughter will ever be her old self. By that I mean she is growing and seeking out her way in this life. You should be prepared for her to change in ways you cannot predict."

Dinah smiled and said, "Vi has never been predictable. When she was just a little thing and I was caring for her, I was always aware of how deeply she felt things. I truly hope that being here has helped to ease her sadness, for all of you have lightened our days."

# Violet's Hidden Doubts

"I wish we had much more time," Elsie mused. "But we must leave the city this afternoon. James will conduct the sabbath service at the plantation church, so we have to reach Viamede by tomorrow night."

"My daddy always said that a wise man tries on a hat before he buys it," Mr. Carpenter answered with a knowing smile. "I believe you want to make sure that this hat will fit the congregation at Viamede. I do hope it's a good fit because Mr. Keith's a fine Christian man with an open mind and a loving heart. He'll make a good chaplain for Viamede."

"It will be a big decision for him," Elsie said. "James came South as a visitor. To make a home here was not in his plans, and he will have to give it careful consideration."

Mr. Carpenter laughed—a deep, warm laugh—and said, "Your remark reminds me of something else my daddy used to say to me whenever I was worrying about some problem or other. He'd say that God does not always take us where we want to go, but He always leads us where we need to be. From what I now know of Mr. Keith, I'm sure that he will be led to the right choice."

# CHAPTER

# Big Decisions at Viamede

*What a man desires is*
*unfailing love....*

PROVERBS 19:22

# Big Decisions at Viamede

*T*he travelers arrived back at Viamede the next day, and on Sunday, James conducted the service for everyone on the plantation. That very evening, after meeting with the elders of the congregation, Elsie and her father asked Cousin James to join them in the library. When Elsie offered him the position of chaplain, James accepted without the slightest pause.

"I am delighted!" declared Horace. "The immediacy of your response tells me that you have already given thought to this possibility."

"I feared you might be unwilling to make a permanent move to the South," Elsie said.

"I have given it much thought and prayer," James said seriously. "Believe me, Cousin Elsie, that my answer to you may be quick, but it comes with a great deal of prayer and self-examination. I just hope I can live up to the standards set by Mr. Mason."

"But you accepted so swiftly that I was not able to tell you the terms of your service," Elsie smiled. "Let me call for coffee, and then we shall go over the details."

She walked to the door of the library, then stopped and looked at her little watch before turning back to her cousin. "By the way," she said, "Mr. Embury and several other members of the church are scheduled to arrive here in about an hour. I believe they also have an offer to discuss with you, Cousin James."

"Two congregations in one day," Horace laughed. "I hope you know what you're getting yourself into, my boy."

By mid-June, the Masons were happily packing for their move to St. Louis, and James, though still the guest of Mr. Embury, was planning to move to Viamede.

Vi's family intended to return to Ion and The Oaks in another month. In the meantime, they settled into the leisurely ways of summer in the Deep South. Lunch was often served under the shade trees in the garden. Hammocks were strung, and the younger members of the family gathered on the lawn in the afternoons—reading, napping, or just lazing. Ice cream, they all joked, had become a necessity, and the twins could often be found on the kitchen steps, taking turns at the hard work of cranking the wooden churn that produced the chilled delicacy.

The sun hung over the flat Delta country well into the early evening, but as it finally dipped behind the treetops, the temperature fell slightly and human energies rose. Fireflies appeared, blinking and darting through the thin mist that rose from the river and inviting the people to shake off their torpor and come out and play.

"I almost hate to call them to bed," Elsie said one evening as she and Molly were sitting on the porch. The twins and Rosemary played in the garden, where candles burned in wrought iron lanterns that lined the garden paths. "They so enjoy running about after the day's heat."

"I remember running like that," Molly said in a strange tone. "I remember the feeling of summer breezes pulling at my hair as I ran and thinking that I could reach the ends of the earth if I just kept going."

Elsie said nothing at first. She had been concerned about Molly lately. After returning from New Orleans, Elsie

noticed that Molly was quieter than usual and distracted almost to absentmindedness at times. That night, Molly had eaten little and said even less at supper. Elsie had assumed the cause was the late tea Molly and Enna had enjoyed with the Emburys at their home, Magnolia Hall, where they had become frequent visitors. Now she wondered.

"Are you feeling well, Molly?" Elsie asked. "This heat can be oppressive, and some days I feel almost feverish from it."

"It is not the heat that oppresses me," Molly replied almost curtly, "nor even the mosquitoes," she added, smacking away one of the pesky creatures that had landed on her bare arm.

"Forgive me, Cousin Elsie," she said a moment later. "Maybe it is the heat that makes me short-tempered tonight." She paused, then exclaimed, "No! That's not true!"

"But what is it, dear Molly?" Elsie asked, for the emotion in her cousin's voice now gave her serious concern.

Molly drew in a deep breath, then let it out in an anguished rush. "Mr. Embury has asked me to marry him," she said, her voice breaking on the word "marry."

Elsie knew instantly not to express her pleasure at this news. She reached out and took Molly's trembling hand. In the pale light from the parlor window, Elsie could see only the outline of Molly's profile, but she instinctively felt the pain the young woman was in.

"What did you tell him?" she asked, keeping her voice low and steady.

"Nothing," Molly answered. "Rather, I told him I would have my answer tomorrow. What a coward I am! I had not the courage to deny his proposal."

"Then you do not love him?"

"I *do* love him! And that's my tragedy! That is why I must refuse him, Elsie. He needs a real wife and a mother to his children—not a helpless invalid!"

"Does he love you?"

"Yes, I truly believe so."

"Why do you believe so?" Elsie asked.

"Because I know the look of pity. I see it often enough," Molly said with a trace of bitterness in her voice. "Yet I know the look of kindness as well, dear cousin. The kindness of real friends. When I look into Mr. Embury's eyes, I see not pity but kindness and something else that I had not expected. You'd think that I, whose life is devoted to words, could describe the look of love, but I cannot. I can only say that I see it in his eyes."

Elsie squeezed Molly's hand. "Mr. Embury does not strike me as the kind of man who would offer marriage out of sympathy."

"But that's the point, Elsie!" Molly cried. "His proposal is genuine! And what I feel for him is genuine. I *want* to be his wife, but I can't! I just can't! And I must tell him that I can't!"

*Oh, Edward, what would you say to her?* Elsie thought frantically. And the answer came as clearly as if he were whispering in her ear.

Elsie said with firmness, "You must make a decision, and you cannot make it if you indulge in this self-pity. God has given you a mind that is the envy of us all. You have the power to reason and pray your way through this, if you do not let yourself give way to self-indulgent emotions."

"How can you say—" Molly tried to interrupt, but Elsie would not allow protest.

"It has been a very long time since I heard you call yourself an invalid, and I do not like the sound of it," Elsie

said, amazing herself at the seeming cruelty of her words. Still she went on: "It seems clear that Mr. Embury does not want to marry out of pity. So ask yourself what he loves. A woman—a *woman*, Molly—with a brilliant talent, a generous and forgiving spirit, and true faith in the love of our Heavenly Father. You are not your handicap, but if you choose to regard yourself as less than a complete person, then it may be true that you do not deserve Mr. Embury's love and affection."

"But Elsie," Molly declared, the old strength and determination returning to her voice. "How can I take on the responsibilities for his daughters, when I am confined to this chair? He already has two children who depend on him; he does not need a third."

"Can you love? Can you listen? Can you caress a child's hair and kiss away tears? Can you teach by your example and correct when necessary? Can you raise a child to know God's love and live by His commandments? These are the things that a parent—a mother—does, dear Molly, and all of them can be accomplished from a seated position."

This last comment drew a smile from Molly. "You sound exactly like Cousin Edward," she said.

"Good!" Elsie responded with a loud sigh. "If I sound like him, then I am saying what is right. I believe he would also say that this decision is one of the most important you will make in your life. You must consider your own happiness as well as Mr. Embury's. You have for so long assumed that marriage was impossible for you that, I fear, the idea has become a truth in your mind. But is it really true?

"Think, Molly. Think of the men who came back from the War with missing limbs and broken bodies. Think of dear Charles Howard who lost his arm and Mr. Graham

who lost his sight and Mr. Winslow who lost both his legs. Are they any less men for their losses? Do your Aunt Lora and Mrs. Graham and Mrs. Winslow love their husbands any less for their physical disabilities? Do their children suffer from lack of adequate fathers?

"Marriage is a union of body, mind, soul, and spirit, Molly. Frankly, if your only concern is the crippled state of your legs, then, yes, perhaps you should turn down this proposal. Mr. Embury deserves better. But I know you, and you are not one to anticipate only the worst of outcomes or to wallow in self-pity."

Softly, Molly said, "You're right, cousin. I did that once, and now I should know better. I even discussed this very thing with Vi after Cousin Edward's accident."

Gently, Elsie responded, "I would never have said what I just did if I thought you weak and self-absorbed. But we all need reminders at times to trust the better parts of our natures. You have a decision to make, and you must consider many factors, of which your handicap is but one. Because I love and respect you, I don't want you to look back on your choice—whatever it may be—with any regret. I want you to talk it over now with the Lord. Take it all to Him. Let Him be your sounding board, and He will help you understand the possibilities."

For a few moments, in the darkness, nothing more was said. Then Elsie heard a familiar noise—the grating of metal and wood against the stone floor of the porch as Molly maneuvered her wheeled chair.

A hand touched Elsie's arm, and Molly said, "I'm going in now. Thank you, Cousin Elsie, for being my friend and speaking honestly. Sleep well tonight, and don't worry about me. I may not be sleeping myself, for I have much to discuss with my Lord. But thanks to you, my head is free of cobwebs. When Louis comes tomorrow morning, I will be able to speak to him with my heart and my head. Whatever my decision, I do not believe that it will be based on false and prideful assumptions."

Elsie lay her own hand atop Molly's and squeezed. "Then it will be the right decision, dearest Molly."

Molly didn't join the family at breakfast the next morning, but only Elsie guessed the reason. The others assumed simply that Molly was eating with her mother and that they would see their cousin later. In the meantime, they talked excitedly about the day's big event—Cousin James was moving in. And they were not the only ones excited by their cousin's arrival.

At breakfast, Horace received a letter that had come from Wealthy Stanhope, his charmingly eccentric and now quite elderly aunt who lived in Lansdale, Ohio. Miss Stanhope was the half-sister of Horace Dinsmore's mother and also the beloved aunt of James and all the Keith children.

Horace read the letter to the family.

*I am so glad to hear that our young James will be ministering there*, Aunt Wealthy wrote in her large, spidery hand. *It's high time my dear Dinsmores and Keiths become kissing cousins again. Distance has separated the two halves of my family for too long, though James will now be more distant from us but closer to you. But I am almost a hundred years away from next June, so Louisiana does not seem so far as it once did.*

After reading the paragraph, Horace looked up and was not at all surprised by the looks of confusion on his grandchildren's faces.

Chuckling, Horace said, "Your great-great-aunt is a most remarkable woman with her own distinctive style of expression."

"But what does she mean by 'a hundred years away'?" Herbert asked.

"She means that next June, she will celebrate her one hundredth birthday," Horace explained. "It has been quite some time since we last saw her," he mused, more to himself than the others. "And longer since we last visited Lansdale."

"Might we go there sometime?" Vi asked. "I've never been to Ohio. It would be exciting!"

"Perhaps we might," Horace agreed. "At least it is an idea for Rose, Elsie, and I to discuss. But we have other things to attend to now. Have you children forgotten that your Cousin James is arriving soon? Mr. Embury will be driving him over, and I expect them within the half hour. So finish your breakfast, and then we will form our welcoming committee."

The family was so busy greeting Cousin James that no one, save Elsie, noticed when Mr. Embury slipped away from the happy throng. Not many minutes later, she saw him on the veranda at the side of the house. He was pushing Molly's chair, and Elsie watched as the pair moved to a shady spot near the railing. Mr. Embury sat on a bench and bent toward Molly. With a small prayer for them both, Elsie turned away and went inside.

About an hour later, Elsie sought out Mrs. O'Flaherty and found her in the pantry. Elsie's purpose was to inform the housekeeper that the family would have their midday meal in the dining room. It would be a larger group than usual, for James would now take a permanent place at their table. Enna, who usually ate separately with her nurse, would be there, and Mr. Embury was to be a guest.

"It's a gathering fit for an announcement, is it not?" Mrs. O'Flaherty said.

Elsie smiled. "Do you read minds?" she asked.

"No, ma'am," Mrs. O'Flaherty said, her blue eyes crinkling at their corners. "Some say we Irish have the gift of second-sight, but that is just blarney. I think we may have a talent for reading hearts, all the same. I have observed Miss Molly and Mr. Embury for some weeks now. And not many minutes ago, I saw them going into the library with Mr. Dinsmore, and the pair of them smiling from ear to ear."

"Ah," Elsie sighed knowingly. She had spoken briefly to the couple, just before their meeting with Horace, so she said, "You have read their hearts correctly, Mrs. O'Flaherty. They are engaged."

"I don't want to go putting the cart before the horse," Mrs. O'Flaherty went on, "but should we begin making plans for a wedding?"

"I believe that would be appropriate," Elsie replied. "An intimate wedding for the families. That is the couple's wish, for Molly dearly wants us here for her nuptials. Do you think we can manage all the preparations within three weeks?"

"We could manage within three days if that were the dear girl's wish," Mrs. O'Flaherty replied confidently.

"No, no. Three weeks will be adequate," Elsie laughed. "We will need that amount of time for Molly's brother to arrange his trip from Philadelphia."

"The young doctor?" Mrs. O'Flaherty asked.

"Indeed, the young doctor," Elsie agreed. Then she suddenly took the woman's hand and shook it heartily. "The young *doctor*!" she exclaimed. Turning on her heel, Elsie gathered up her skirts and rushed away, calling back over her shoulder, "Thank you very, *very* much, Mrs. O'Flaherty!"

A few days later, a telegraph message arrived from Philadelphia. Dick Percival would reach Viamede in time to give his sister's hand in marriage. Enna and Molly were overjoyed at the prospect of Dick's arrival. He had come to Ion for Edward's funeral the previous October, but that visit with his family had been brief and steeped in sadness.

Mr. Mason and Cousin Jame happily agreed to perform the marriage service, which would take place in Viamede's formal parlor. Missy and Vi would attend Molly as bridesmaids, and Horace would stand as Mr. Embury's best man. The family and their few guests would enjoy a wedding feast in the upstairs ballroom — a room that had not known gaiety since the days when Elsie's grandparents had entertained there nearly a half-century earlier. Mrs. O'Flaherty saw to it that Viamede was polished from top to bottom. But Aunt Mamie, in much better health now, insisted on supervising the kitchen duties and making the wedding cakes herself.

Through all the hurried preparations, Molly was a marvel of patience and concern for others. She was especially solicitous of her mother and of Mr. Embury's daughters. The two little girls were invited to stay at Viamede as often as they liked, and Molly made time each day to be alone

with Corinne and Maddie. Thus were the foundations of their relationship laid. As for Enna, the little girls took to her immediately and had soon christened her "Grannie Enna."

# CHAPTER 17

# Growing Toward God

*And we pray this in order that you may live a life worthy of the LORD…growing in the knowledge of God….*

COLOSSIANS 1:10

One evening early in the week of the wedding, Molly invited Vi to join her in the garden after supper. The other girls each had something important to attend to, so it was just Molly and Vi who adjourned to a pretty little spot beside a small, bubbling fountain near the rear of the house.

"I'm going to miss you, Vi," Molly began, "more than you know."

"That's nice of you to say, but I doubt you'll have time to miss any of us," Vi replied in a teasing tone. "A new husband, new home, two sweet children, plus your writing—goodness, Molly, your days will be full to overflowing."

"That doesn't mean I won't miss you," Molly said. "I wanted us to have some private time, so I asked the others not to join us tonight."

"Oh, that explains—" Vi began.

"All those pressing duties that weighed so on Missy and Isa? Yes, it was my request," Molly continued. "I wanted us to have a chance to talk as we have so often. Do you remember when I first came to live at Ion?"

"Of course I remember. I thought you and Dick the most mature 'young' people I'd ever known. I loved to be around you, and I made a pest of myself, I'm sure."

"Not at all, dear Vi. Everyone in your family was so gracious and kind to us, but did you know that you were my favorite? You would come to my room every morning, rain or shine. You still had your baby curls then, and you would bounce about my room as if you were on springs. No matter how foul my mood, you always managed to chase it away

when you visited me. You were the first person, child or adult, since my accident who took no special notice of my crippled legs. You knew that I couldn't walk, and you asked me why."

"I don't remember that," Vi said.

"You asked. I explained. And that was the end of it. You weren't afraid of me, or pitying, or even sympathetic. You simply accepted me. As I began to lose my anger and struggled to think of myself as a true child of God, I looked to your example."

Molly paused for a moment, then quoted from Scripture, " 'And a little child will lead them.' Without knowing it, you led me as I learned to accept myself, limitations and all."

"That was a long time ago," Vi said softly.

"It was, but I have a feeling that you might like to know how you have influenced me."

Darkness was falling and Vi could barely see her cousin's face, but she felt Molly's hand on her wrist.

"You and I have much in common beyond kinship," Molly said. "We are different in ways that can sometimes make us uncomfortable. It's too easy for people like us to doubt ourselves. We may be tempted to think ourselves alone or to blame ourselves for things we cannot control. I'm saying this to you because I have recently been made aware, once again, of this inclination in myself."

"You said something like that before," Vi replied, "on the day of Papa's accident."

"I just wanted you to know that you aren't alone in your feelings. You'll never be alone as long as God's love lives in your heart." Molly sat back in her chair. Then she asked, "How do you feel about growing up?"

Vi's first response was a heavy sigh. She gathered her thoughts and finally said, "Confused. I want to grow up.

There are so many things that I want to do that I cannot now. Yet a part of me wants to remain as I am—to stay always at Ion with Mamma and let her guide me and be there for me. Did you ever feel that way, Molly?"

"Well, my Mamma was not an ideal parent, but yes, at times. Circumstances forced me to grow up faster than I wanted, but I fought against it. If your mother and father had not been there for me, I might still be the selfish and self-pitying child who arrived at Ion. Now, I can look back and understand myself and others so much better. I can see that Mamma always loved Dick and me. She was misguided in her goals and often thoughtless of our feelings, but she never meant to hurt us. When I was a child, everyone seemed so simple to me. There were either masters or slaves, rich or poor, young or old. But as I opened my heart to God, I learned that every life is complicated. I began to value and love other people for their differences. And I also began to see myself as a whole person—although I still have a tendency to focus too much on my handicap," Molly added, thinking of her conversation with Elsie on the night before she accepted Mr. Embury's proposal.

"I'm conscious of your chair, but I don't think of you as handicapped or disabled," Vi said.

"Because you look into my heart, dear Vi," Molly said, "and that is one of your gifts. It is a gift that you should cultivate and train—as you would a flowering vine—so that it serves others and glorifies the Giver of all gifts. What sets you apart, what you call difference, comes from the Lord, but it is up to you to make the most of it."

Vi didn't say anything, but she was grappling with the import of Molly's words.

# Violet's Hidden Doubts

"Oh, dear," Molly said after several uncomfortable moments. "I must sound like a terrible old busybody telling you how to live your life."

"No, you don't! Not at all," Vi protested. "I know that I've been concentrating too much on all the sadness of the last year. What you said about little children, the way they see things in simple terms—I've been thinking that way, and it doesn't work. I want to strive to be more like my Papa. He found value in every person. He wasn't afraid of complicated problems and being responsible for himself and others."

"Your father could look back and learn," Molly said. "He could look forward and plan and dream. But he never forgot where he was. Four days from now, I will leave all of you to make my own home and family, but I have wonderful examples to guide me. When I'm unsure of myself, I can turn in my mind to Cousin Edward and his model of wisdom and compassion. I can turn to Cousin Elsie, so steadfast in faith and love. I can think of you, dear Vi, and your open heart and questioning mind. I will have each of you to guide me as I choose my own course and set the example for others. God loves me the way I am. But He wants me to continue learning from others even as I follow my heart's desire."

Vi sighed and said, "Growing up doesn't mean that we stop growing, does it? We don't stop learning?"

Molly said, "From our first to our last breath, Vi, God gives us the power to grow in faith, in hope, and in love. We change as we mature and put childish ways behind us. But think of it, Vi. Every day of our lives—even in hardships and trials—we are growing toward God. That is the real adventure, isn't it? It's the trials that help us to mature along the way."

Vi leaned forward and grabbed Molly's hand. "It is a journey," she agreed. "A great and exciting journey! Why have I been afraid to embark on it?"

"Because you're human," Molly replied. "But our Lord has shown us the way. Think about when He walked on the water and His disciples were terrified at seeing Him there. He calmed the wind and made the water smooth. 'Take courage,' he said. 'It is I. Don't be afraid.' He wants us to venture forth with courage, Vi, because He is always there to support us."

The two young women would have talked on well into the night had not Mrs. O'Flaherty come into the garden and politely reminded them of the late hour.

As Vi pushed Molly's chair back toward the house, she said, "I'll miss our talks, Molly. You said earlier that I had influenced you to accept yourself. Well, now you have returned the favor. I will confess something to you. Last month, on the day I turned fifteen, we had that lovely party. It was subdued, of course, but everyone was so happy for me and gave me such nice presents. But when I was alone that night, after my prayers with Mamma, I just cried like a baby until I finally cried myself to sleep. Yet I couldn't have said why I felt sad. Now I wish I could have that birthday over again, so that I could rejoice that I am growing up. I would be able to say, 'I'm fifteen, and I'm growing toward God. I am embarking on the greatest journey of all, and I'm not afraid.'"

"You can't have the birthday back," Molly replied, "but you always have that thought. May I share it with you? I'd like to start each new day with that thought too. Whatever the day may bring, I am growing toward God!"

Vi considered for a moment. "If we both think it, God will hear us," she said, "and it will be as if we are praying together, won't it? Like we are together no matter how far apart we are."

∽

Dick Percival arrived two days before the wedding, and the reunion with his mother and sister was indescribably sweet. Enna could barely allow him to leave her. But on the morning of the wedding, Elsie took her cousin for a walk in the garden.

"Do you approve of your sister's choice of husband?" she asked.

"I do," the young man said. "Their union confirms the wisdom of God's plan, doesn't it? Who would have thought that our Molly would have found her life partner in the bayous of Louisiana?"

"And what do you think of this part of the South?" Elsie asked.

"After so short an acquaintance, my thoughts are hardly worthwhile. Yet I am very happy to be back in the South. I've missed my homeland."

"But don't you intend to stay in Philadelphia?"

"That was my plan," he replied. "I could build a profitable practice and make a name for myself there. Yet what good is money and prestige if physicians do not take their knowledge to those who most need it?"

Then Dick added, "I've been giving much thought to the true meaning of a life of faith. I often turn to the words of Paul in 2 Corinthians 8: 'But just as you excel in everything—in faith, in speech, in knowledge, in complete earnestness and in your love for us—see that you also excel in this grace of giving…. For you know the grace of our Lord Jesus Christ, that though he was rich, yet for your sakes he became poor, so that you through his poverty might become rich.' As a man, Jesus ministered to one and all, without distinction. Isn't His life the example I want to follow?"

Elsie laid her hand on his arm. "And how have you answered your own question?"

"In truth, Cousin Elsie, I've decided not to return to practice in Philadelphia. I want to be a country doctor like Dr. Barton and Cousin Art. I won't be rich. I won't be famous. But I am convinced that my happiness lies elsewhere." He laughed. "Now, I must discover where."

Elsie could have made him an offer then and there. But however much it would please her to have Dick at Viamede, she knew that it would be unfair to take advantage of the moment. She did, however, feel justified in planting one very small seed.

"There is someone I want you to meet," she said as they turned toward the house again. "An old and dear friend to Edward and me. Dr. Bayliss has seen to the health of this parish for many years, and he reminds me a good deal of Dr. Barton. He is retiring soon, and we will greatly miss his conscientious service."

"I should like to meet him," Dick said.

"You shall have your chance at the wedding," Elsie said.

They talked of other matters for the rest of their walk, but unknown to Elsie, an idea very much like her own was beginning to take shape in her young cousin's mind.

191

# Violet's Hidden Doubts

The marriage of Miss Molly Percival and Mr. Louis Embury took place late that afternoon. Although the number of guests was small, the occasion was celebrated with enormous cheer. Except for Elsie, none of the Travillas were now expected to wear the black clothes of mourning. So Vi and Missy were attired in charming pastel frocks as they stood next to Molly, who was beautiful in her new white gown and an antique wedding veil lent to her by Mrs. Mason.

Following the ceremony, the groom carried his bride up the sweeping stairs to Viamede's ballroom. In the center of that large room, beneath the exquisite, Italian crystal chandelier purchased by Elsie's grandmother, tables had been drawn together in a U-shaped arrangement, draped in white damask cloths, and set with elegant French china, crystal, and silverware. Cut-glass bowls filled with pink and white camellias decorated the tables, alternating with silver candelabra holding white tapers. All the gallery doors into the ballroom were open to catch the evening breezes, and the candle flames flickered softly.

The two little Embury girls were seated between their father and new stepmother—comfortable cushions on their chairs raising the children up so they might see and be seen by all.

Aunt Mamie had outdone herself, and the wedding supper was superb. The guests were treated to many of the delicacies of the region including oysters and shrimp fresh from the Gulf, as well as spicy rice and vegetable dishes and an array of cool salads. Dessert included an icy orange confection made from the fruits of Viamede's grove, a variety of cakes, and Mamie's famous lace cookies.

Toasts to the bridal couple were made throughout the meal. Horace began with a prayer of thanks to God for the joys of

family. Then James offered a toast to love (which Vi thought sweet but oddly sentimental for James). Dick filled his remarks with gentle humor and expressed his special pleasure at becoming an uncle to Corinne and Maddie. Then Enna stood, and not a few eyes welled with tears as she spoke lovingly of her daughter, her son-in-law, and her new grandchildren. Her words were simple and brief, ending with a prayer of thanks to "our Savior, who must have loved weddings because He chose a wedding for His first miracle."

The party drew to its close at about nine, when Molly, Louis, their children, and Enna left Viamede for the ride to Magnolia Hall. Enna had accepted the offer to live at Magnolia Hall with the Emburys.

Dr. and Mrs. Bayliss departed soon after the Emburys, but not before receiving Dick's promise to join them for lunch the next day. Dr. Bayliss was most anxious to continue a conversation begun over the supper table with the bright young doctor from Philadelphia.

Vi had thought she would be sad to see Molly go, but in fact, her heart was nearly bursting with joy for her cousin. As the Embury carriage drove away into the night, Vi was thinking how proud her papa would be. *Papa always found his greatest pleasure in the happiness of others,* Vi told herself. *Now I understand why. When one of us is blessed, we are all blessed.*

A verse from Psalm 68 came to her mind, and she offered it as her own private toast to the newlyweds: "But may the righteous be glad and rejoice before God; may they be happy and joyful."

# CHAPTER

## 18

# Messages of Love

*I will give them comfort and
joy instead of sorrow.*

JEREMIAH 31:13

he family were to leave Viamede on the following Monday, and it was with mixed feelings that they completed their packing.

"Did you accomplish everything you needed to, Mamma?" Missy asked.

It was the afternoon after the wedding, and Missy and Vi were enjoying a rare time alone with their mother in the parlor. Dick had gone to the Bayliss home, and the twins were out on a last horseback ride over the plantation. Isa had taken Rosemary and Danny for a romp in the orange grove, and James insisted on accompanying them.

"I believe so," Elsie replied to Missy's question. "Our business enterprises are in excellent hands. Viamede has a new manager and a new chaplain."

"But we didn't find a doctor," Vi said.

"No, but I have confidence that problem may be resolved without our intervention," Elsie replied. "What's more, we have wonderful news to take home to Aunt Chloe and Joe about Dinah and her family."

Vi smiled, thinking of all that she had experienced at the mission. But then she had another, more immediate thought, and she asked, "What of Mrs. O'Flaherty? Will she have to leave Viamede now that Aunt Mamie is so much better?"

"You like Mrs. O'Flaherty very much, don't you?" Elsie asked in return.

"Oh, we do, Mamma. We all do," Vi said enthusiastically. "She's so interesting. She has told us so many things about Ireland and about Louisiana, too." A little frown came to

Vi's face as she added, "I still wish I knew more about her, though."

"Whatever Mrs. O'Flaherty's story, it is hers alone to tell," Elsie said a little firmly. "But you will be glad to know that she will stay on here for as long as she wants. Aunt Mamie will not be capable of returning to her full duties, so Mrs. O'Flaherty has agreed to remain as housekeeper while Mamie manages the kitchen and assists Cousin James to settle in."

The girls were delighted by this news. But with a sigh, Missy said, "It will be strange to return to Ion without Molly and Aunt Enna. Am I very selfish to feel sad at losing them to Mr. Embury?"

"Not at all, dearest," Elsie said. "I would wonder if you did not suffer to some extent from mixed emotions."

"We have had our share of separations this year," Vi said in a wistful tone, and her mother and sister knew that Vi was thinking of her father. For several moments, none of them spoke.

Then Elsie said, perhaps a little too brightly, "Tell me about the presents you received from Molly. She purchased something for each of you girls, but she insisted that her gifts be a secret even from me."

"We hadn't any idea that she had planned such a surprise," Missy said. "Each gift was hidden in a special place for us to find. Mine was in my stationery box." She put her hand to her throat and drew from beneath her blouse a sterling silver pendant on a delicate chain.

"See," she said, holding out the necklace. "It's a locket of the old style. It opens, and Molly left a note telling me to have Lester paint a miniature of himself to fill the frame inside. She was very specific. Lester must paint his image

for me—no photograph—so that I might feel him close whenever I wear it."

Missy leaned forward so that her mother could examine the jewelry.

"What a loving gift," Elsie said, thinking of the small gold locket that she wore always. It contained a miniature of her father and the only image she had of her long-dead mother.

Vi was saying, "Molly gave Isa a book of poems by Mrs. Elizabeth Barrett Browning—*Sonnets from the Portuguese*. She'd marked one with a ribbon—'How do I love thee? Let me count the ways'—and Isa read it out loud to us and got all dreamy. Have you noticed that Isa gets that dreamy look a lot these days? I can't think what's the matter with her."

Elsie smiled but said only, "And what did Molly leave for you, Vi?"

Vi tried to look mysterious but could not hide her dimpled smile as she said, "It's neither silver nor gold. I found it in my bedside table, in the drawer where I keep my Bible."

"A book?" Elsie asked.

"'A book yet to be written.' That's what Molly's note said," Vi replied. "It's a journal, Mamma, just like hers, but the pages are blank, of course. But not completely blank, for Molly wrote out some verses on the very first page. 'You yourselves are our letter, written on our hearts, known and read by everybody.'"

Vi hesitated, and Elsie completed the passage from Second Corinthians, saying, "You show that you are a letter from Christ, the result of our ministry, written not with ink but with the Spirit of the living God, not on tablets of stone but on tablets of human hearts.' That is a wonderful gift, pet. Do you know how Molly uses her journals?"

"She writes down things that happen and ideas for her stories," Vi said.

"That's one use," Elsie agreed. "But Molly has often said to me that her journal is also her ongoing letter to the Lord. She writes her thoughts and prayers there, and she says that writing things down can bring clarity to confusion and help her sort through her ideas. Did you not notice how frequently she retired to her room and her journal in the weeks before her engagement?"

"I did, Mamma, but I never thought of her writing to God," Vi said. She giggled and added, "Then I never thought of her marrying Mr. Embury either."

"There are many means by which we communicate with the Lord," Elsie continued. "So long as we open our hearts freely, it matters not how we speak to Him. He always hears us."

Vi's expression became serious. "I'd like to keep a journal, but I don't know where to start," she said. "I thought about describing Molly's wedding."

"That's a very good beginning," Missy said. "Write about it while the details are fresh in your memory."

"It's for you to decide, Vi dear," Elsie said, "what to write and if you wish to write at all. Molly would not want you to regard her gift as a duty. She wanted to share with each of us something that has meaning for her. I am greatly impressed by her choices, for each gift was clearly selected with personal consideration. Even in the whirlwind of her wedding preparations, Molly was thinking of us."

Vi caught her mother's use of the word "us," and she asked, "Did Molly give you a present too, Mamma?"

"She did, and it is one I shall always cherish," Elsie replied in a soft tone. "I found it tucked in my Bible. It is a

letter that your papa wrote to Molly when she and Dick first came to live at Ion nearly a decade ago. Your father wrote to ask if she would allow him to act in the role of father to her. Molly must have read it often, for its pages are worn by being unfolded and folded many times. I would like you both to hear your Papa's letter, for she asks me to share it with the family."

"Do you have it with you, Mamma?" Vi asked.

"No, pet. Molly put it in my Bible, and I think that is where it belongs. But if you like, we can go up to my room now and read it."

Open trunks and travel cases crowded Elsie's lovely bedroom, but after taking her Bible from the dressing table, she moved aside some clothing that lay across her favorite chair and took her seat. Missy and Vi settled comfortably on the bed as Elsie opened the Bible and carefully withdrew a yellowed envelope. Taking out the pages, she said, "It is dated in the fall of 1870," and she began to read Edward's letter.

Dear Molly,

When I first decided to write, it was because I was full of sound advice and sage words. But I have thought better. If you wish to seek my counsel on any matter, I am here for you. But you are a wise young woman, and both Elsie and I credit you with a great deal more common sense than either of us possessed at your age. I could not feel more proud of you than if you were my very own child.

# Violet's Hidden Doubts

You had little chance to know your own father. May I tell you something about him? Your brother's namesake was, as a boy, what is often called "a handful" with a penchant for mischief. You have, I know, heard many stories of his youthful escapades. You have also been told, unfairly I believe, of his misdeeds. But I want to tell you about what was admirable.

Your father made mistakes but was unerringly honest in owning up to them. He was extremely intelligent and, you may be surprised to learn, a great reader, for his curiosity was unquenchable. He was profligate with money, yet he was equally generous, and his financial losses were often the result of loans to others in need. His contemporaries still speak of your father as the most loyal of friends. He was, beyond question, a man of true courage. He fought bravely in the Civil War and was unafraid to face death when it came. Most important, your father loved Enna and you and young Dick with his whole heart. Of that truth, you must never doubt.

I, like you, lost my father before I was old enough to really know him. I understand what it is like to wonder about the kind of person he was. Dear Molly, I see in you and in your brother all that was good in your father—the brave and independent spirit, the inquisitive mind and goodhearted generosity, the honesty and loyalty. He did not store up wealth for you, but from him you inherited other gifts more precious than gold.

I would never attempt to take his place, but I wish to offer you the love of a fatherly friend—as your Papa would surely have done if our roles were reversed. I have a willing ear for listening and broad shoulders to bear weighty problems. I am tall enough so that, on occasion, I can peer above the trees to see the wide forest. Though some may dispute it, my sense of humor is rather acute, and I sense that you are a girl with considerable laughter in her heart. I am at times insightful and have a well-developed sense of justice and fairness (quite useful when negotiating spats between siblings). These qualifications will, I hope, recommend me to your service.

You would pay me a great compliment if you accept my offer. In part, I may help make up for the injustice done to you by the slanders on your father's memory. But more important is the opportunity you can give me to love and support you as your own father would have. But if surrogate parenthood is too lofty a position to seek, I will love and support you nonetheless. Like it or not, Miss Molly Percival, I intend always to be your most loyal friend and your devoted,

*Cousin Edward*

Elsie placed the letter on the table beside her and took up several more sheets of paper—these as white and fresh as the first letter was timeworn. "This is the rest of Molly's gift to me," Elsie said to her daughters, and she began to read aloud again.

Dearest Cousin Elsie,

I was just fourteen and recently moved to Ion when Cousin Edward wrote to me. I was still in a state of turmoil then—plagued by doubts and fears, and worst of all, self-hatred, for I had not yet learned to value myself as a child of God. I was even frightened by your

family's Christian faith, for your lives seemed so full and mine so empty and hopeless.

I don't know what impelled Cousin Edward to write as he did, but his letter came like a spring thaw for my frozen heart. Somehow he understood that part of my suffering could be traced to my fears that I was like my father, who had always been portrayed to me as willful, self-indulgent, and irresponsible. As I later told Cousin Edward — after I accepted his offer of friendly fatherhood — one of my earliest memories is of the day we learned that my father was dead. I was very young, yet I remember Grandmother Dinsmore saying over and over, "It's for the best. He was a bad lot, a bad lot." I remember thinking that if my Papa was so bad, then I must be, too.

Cousin Edward was the first person who ever told me that my own father, for all his faults, was not a bad person. Somehow Cousin Edward knew that I needed to learn about my father if I was to begin to free myself from my terrible self-doubt. By writing forthrightly of my father and then offering his own love and support, he showed me a kind of respect that I had never experienced. Eventually, I came to regard his letter as a reminder of what it means to care for a person so much — even a person as difficult as I was then — that you are willing to look into the dark part of her and bring in light.

You will see by its tattered condition how often I have returned to Cousin Edward's letter. Now I want you to have it. When you spoke to me on the night before I accepted Louis's proposal, it was with the same uncanny understanding that Cousin Edward showed when he wrote his letter. Please share this gift with my beloved

cousins if you like, for I carry you all in my heart as I go forward on this new path God has opened to me.

*I love you,*
*Molly*

Elsie looked up and smiled at Vi. "Your cousin added a postscript for you, pet. She writes, 'I think Vi will especially understand her father's letter to me. He gave me a piece of my past so that I might grow toward my future.' Do you take her meaning, dear?"

"Yes, Mamma," Vi said. "It is something that Molly and I talked about."

"But, Mamma, what was it you said to Molly?" Missy asked.

"Oh, I simply reminded her of some plain truths," Elsie replied vaguely. "I don't remember my exact words. Yet I can tell you that I felt as if your father were standing at my shoulder the whole time."

Vi had picked up her father's letter and was reading it to herself. She was about to turn to the second page when she looked up at her mother and said, "May I borrow this for the rest of the afternoon, Mamma? I shall be very careful with it."

"Of course, darling," Elsie replied, "but may I inquire what you plan to do?"

Vi smiled softly, her dimple showing. "I have decided to start my journal by copying this letter into it," she said.

"That's a nice idea," Missy said, "but wouldn't you rather start with your own words?"

Vi looked at her sister, then her mother, and Elsie saw in her daughter's expressive face and sparkling eyes a look so like Edward's that she lost her breath for an instant.

"These *are* my words, in a way," Vi answered. "Molly kept Papa's letter all these years as a reminder of him, and now she

has given it to us. If I write it out in my journal, I will have it always. I can read Papa's letter and remember what it means to love someone so much that you are willing to look into the darkness and bring in light. Isn't that what Molly said, Mamma?"

"It is, my darling," Elsie said.

"And that will remind me to do what is *really* right for others," Vi continued. "And to think—*really* think—about what people need. That's what Mr. Carpenter advised me to do. That's what Papa did, and what you do for all of us, Mamma. That's what Jesus did when He went out to teach and to heal. That's what God wants all of us to do for one another. But it's hard for me sometimes because I think too much about what *I* want and how *I* feel. Isn't it amazing that Papa understood what was hurting Molly when no one else did? And when you read his letter, Mamma, it was as if he were talking to us. So whenever I read it again, I will hear his voice as if he were still teaching me, and his words will remind me how important it is to be more understanding of others."

Vi, her face flushing with the excitement of her new insight, asked, "May I go copy this now, Mamma, before the others return? Then you can share it with them, too."

"Yes, dear, go to your work," Elsie said. And Vi hurried away, holding her father's letter before her as if it were a king's jeweled crown.

Vi was gone, but both Elsie and Missy continued to gaze at the open door as if they had just seen some startling sight that lingered on in their vision.

"My little sister is growing up," Missy said at last in a near-whisper. "I had not noticed until just now how much she has changed. She is very like Papa, isn't she?"

"Very like," Elsie replied. "Our fairy child is growing up, and I sense that she is beginning to look forward to the prospect."

"I wonder what she will do with her life," Missy said. "I have the feeling that whatever her path, it will not be predictable."

"Mr. Carpenter said that very thing to me when we were in New Orleans," Elsie replied in some surprise. "And your father often remarked that all our children must leave the nest, but Vi may have to fly farther for her happiness."

Missy thought for a moment then said, "She has Papa's spirit as well as his looks."

Elsie looked away from the door and toward her eldest child. Smiling, she said, "And you, my dear Missy, have more than your share of his wisdom."

Missy laughed happily. "I hope I have an equal portion of yours, Mamma," she said, "for then I shall be very wise indeed. Now, how may I help you?"

There were a few things left to be done, and as Missy and Elsie packed, they talked about their plans for the next day, which included church service and a final visit to the little cemetery where Elsie's mother and grandparents lay. But their conversation was interrupted when Vi danced into the room.

"Are you finished with your copying so soon?" Elsie said.

"Almost," Vi replied. "But I just had to ask you something, Mamma. What would you think if I wore my hair up? After all, I am fifteen now and as tall as you. It's time I looked my age, don't you think?"

"It is something to consider," Elsie replied, turning her head to hide her smile.

"Something to consider," Vi said gravely. She walked to her mother's mirror and looked at her reflection. She

twisted her shoulder-length tresses into a neat chignon, a few dark wisps trailing against her long, graceful neck. She moved her head slowly from one side to the other. She was finally seeing something that she never had before — in her brown eyes, her well-shaped mouth, her straight nose and firm chin, even in the dark sleekness of her hair. She was seeing her Papa's legacy to her, visible now in her appearance, but so much more valuable for what he had left in her heart.

*This business of growing up is really not so hard,* she thought. *I can almost hear Papa laughing and telling me to get on with it before I am too old to leave the nest. Then he would hug my shoulder and tell me not to be afraid of what the future may bring, for my best Friend in Heaven and on earth is with my every step and will catch me if I stumble. Whatever the day may bring, I am growing toward God.*

After a few more moments of contemplation, she said in an unnaturally deep voice, "Yes, I definitely think a change of style would do me good. I will wear my hair up and perhaps try a corset on occasion."

At that, Missy burst into laughter. "You want to wear a corset?" she exclaimed. "You are a silly goose, Violet Travilla!"

Vi turned away from the mirror — her expression set like stone but her eyes sparkling with merriment. "A goose today," she said. "But who knows, dear sister, what I may become tomorrow?"

**An unexpected invitation
leads Vi to distant places.**

**What awaits her? How far
must she go to help a loved one?**

Violet's story continues in:

# VIOLET'S AMAZING SUMMER

Book Two
of the
*A Life of Faith:
Violet Travilla* Series

## A Life of Faith: Violet Travilla Series

# Collect all of our Elsie products!

## A Life of Faith: Elsie Dinsmore Series

## * Now Available as a Dramatized Audiobook!

# Collect all of our Millie products!

**❋ Now Available as a Dramatized Audiobook!**

# Beloved Literary Characters
## *Come to Life!*

*Y*our favorite heroines, Millie Keith, Elsie Dinsmore, Violet Travilla, Laylie Colbert, and Kathleen McKenzie are now available as lovely designer dolls from Mission City Press.

*M*ade of soft-molded vinyl, these beautiful, fully-jointed 18¾" dolls come dressed in historically-accurate clothing and accessories. They wonderfully reflect the Biblical virtues that readers have come to know and love about Millie, Elsie, Violet, Laylie, and Kathleen.

For more information, visit www.alifeoffaith.com or check with your local Christian retailer.

## A Life of Faith® Products from Mission City Press—

### *"It's Like Having a Best Friend From Another Time"*

# Check out our web site at
## www.alifeoffaith.com!

- Find out about all the *A Life of Faith* role models
- Get news about the time periods they lived in
- Learn to live a life of faith like them
- Find out about *A Life of Faith* products
- Explore page after page of inspiring advice to help you grow in your relationship with God!

### www.alifeoffaith.com

## *Ordinary Girls • Extraordinary Faith*

# What Readers are Saying...

### Heidi, age 15
After reading the Violet books, I felt better about growing up. Some girls seem to "have it all together," and I don't. I feel so inadequate sometimes. Reading the Violet books, especially "Violet's Hidden Doubts," helped me trust God more, knowing that even though I feel out of control, God's in control of everything, and will help me. He will never give me more than I can bear. Thank you for writing the Violet books!

### Chantelle, age 14
Violet has an amazingly strong faith in the trials she goes through. Following her life story, even though fictional, is a wonderful adventure for any reader. I look forward to seeing what Vi does with her life!

### Taylor, age 13
I have read all the Millie, Elsie, and the Violet books that have been released. I love to read and when I read these books it's like being in that time period. When I got the first Violet book I read it overnight! These books are so good, and when someone asks me what my favorite books are I say the A Life of Faith series!!!

### Kelly, age 12
I respect Violet so much as she goes through hard times. She has such courage and strength.

### Ashley, age 11
The Violet books are wonderful! They have many life lessons in them. I really enjoy reading about someone so young having so much faith and courage. She is an inspiration to us all.

### Hannah, age 10
They are the best books in the world! I can't wait until the other books come out. I LOVE them all! I love the series so much; I can't explain it in ordinary words!!!!!!!!!